In memory of Jim.

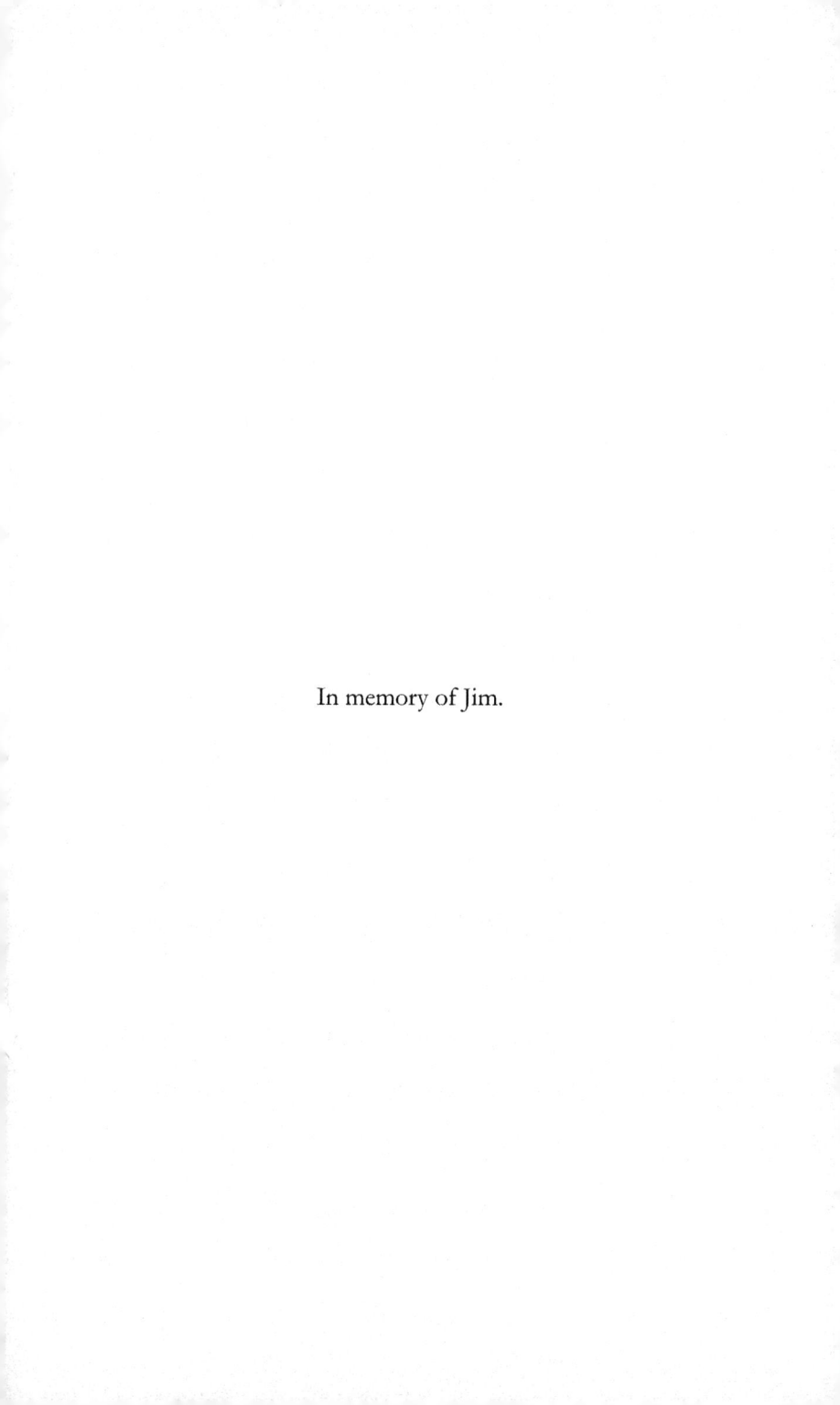

PART 1

"...there in the open plain below I saw two marble statues, one of them, you'd swear, in flight, the other pouncing on its prey. Some god, if gods were watching, must have willed that both should be unbeaten in that chase."

-Ovid

ONE

Light poked through the trees of the dark woods. It was morning, and the cool mist was beginning to dissipate. Deep greens blanketed an old, moss-covered log. The quiet was broken up by the sounds of crackling sticks as a small red fox jumped onto the log. A big, fluffy dog followed behind.

"How long have we been doing this?" the fox said as he jumped from the log and stepped into the clearing. He needed to catch his breath.

"Time is a wheel," the dog answered, rolling on his back and showing his belly to the sky.

"Time is a wheel," the fox muttered, rolling his eyes.

He walked over and plopped down next to the dog, rolling over in the same fashion, belly to the sky.

"I love the sky and the sunshine," the fox said.

"Says the Ruler of Darkness," the dog replied.

"You can be a real dick sometimes, you know it?"

The dog shrugged.

"Thirty-two names," the fox continued, "Don't you think that's overkill? I have thirty-two different names. All of 'em bad. No one ever thought to call me 'The

Sexual Dynamo' or 'Mr. Easy Breezy' or something cool like that. No, it's always 'Hey, there goes the Lawless One' or 'Thief' or 'Prince of the Power of the Air,' which I don't even get…"

"If the names fit," the dog said.

"How many names do you have?"

"I have no need for names. I am all the names, and none of the names," the dog answered.

"Yeah, but if you had to choose a name what would it be?"

"Oh, I don't know… maybe 'Gary.'"

"GARY?! No, no no… You can't pick 'Gary,' it has to be something badass!"

"I like 'Gary.'"

"No way. It has to have some sparkle, man. It's gotta pop."

"Okay…" the dog took a moment to think, "I would be 'The Gold Wizard!'"

"The Gold Wizard?"

"Yes, now that's a name that pops. It's perfect."

"Maybe 'The Chode Wizard,'" the fox said under his breath.

"What?"

"Huh? Oh nothing. Yeah, that's a good name. Sparkly."

They relaxed in the wet grass for a bit, staring into the blue above them. They were somewhere in southern America, but they had been all over the world at this point; a seemingly endless chase.

"Seriously, how long has it been?" the fox asked.

"A very long time."

"Let's just call it. It's okay to be wrong. Just admit it."

"I'm not wrong."

"You still haven't caught me."

"You'll see how it all works out."

"I've been thinking of a different game, anyway," the fox said. He stretched out his legs. Clouds were moving across the sky. It felt good to slow down.

"Oh? What is this other game you're talking about?" the dog asked.

"Well, the lord can do all things right? I'm talking ALL THINGS here... He can make the impossible possible?" the fox said.

"This again? Yes... of course."

"I still haven't been caught..."

"Soon you will understand. What's the game?"

"Can the all powerful and omnipotent lord... who can do ALL things....with no bounds... create a locked door that even he could never open?"

"Of course," The dog answered.

"I'll believe it when I see it."

The fox jumped up and darted back into the woods. The fluffy dog stood up, shook off the dew, and continued the chase.

*   *   *   *   *

It was New Year's Eve, 1985, and Colin Lodestar didn't know it yet, but was about to have burnt eggs for dinner. It was a clear night in eastern Colorado, and Colin was out on his porch of his family farmhouse drinking a beer and looking at the stars.

Colin was going into the New Year with aspirations of an existential overhaul, of personal growth. He was ready to try new things and take on more challenges. He was ready to face the New Year with his chest out. However, he would settle for just finding a girlfriend.

He was in love once, long ago. Anna. She was bold and adventurous and fun and caring. He admired her. They were traits that he wished he had, himself.

He looked up at the big dipper. He loved the constellations as a kid. He would sit outside on this very porch and sketch them in crayon. You could cook a lot of eggs in that pan. Eggs.

"SHIT, MY EGGS!" he remembered.

He ran inside and quickly moved the frying pan off of the burner. It was smoky, and the scent of hot metal drifted through the kitchen.

"Dammit!" he said as he scraped the crispy eggs onto a plate.

It was a forced meal, but growing up on the farm instilled the importance of not wasting your food.

He had lived on the cattle farm his whole life. His father had been dead for over ten years now, and his mother had passed away a few years back, leaving the farm and all of the chores to him. He thought many times about just selling it all and moving somewhere else. He could go to Denver. Hell, he could go anywhere, but he couldn't bring himself to part with it just yet. It was the only home he knew.

Colin finished his dinner with a long drink of beer and put the can in the sink. It was a holiday, so he decided to crack another one.

He was interrupted by a commotion from the chickens out back. He walked out the backdoor to check on them. The porch light barely reached the pen, however, the moonlight was reflecting off of the snow illuminating the yard with a faint glow. He found a trail of strange foot prints leading from the back of the pen, toward the other side of the house.

"What the heck are these?"

He went back to the house to grab his twelve-gauge shotgun.

Coyotes. He had never seen tracks like that before, but couldn't think of anything else.

He loaded the shotgun and reached for the door, but before he could open it, it was ripped from the hinges.

Colin froze in terror when he saw the monster. He was easily eight feet tall and drool oozed down its teeth. Its eyes drilled through Colin. It was pure evil.

Colin didn't even aim the shotgun, he just fired in the monster's direction.

"Agh, my balls!" the monster cried out as he fell to the ground.

Colin couldn't believe what was happening. He was paralyzed by fear and confusion.

The monster stopped writhing and stood back up, towering over the man.

"Just kidding," the creature giggled, "I'm a demon from Hell! You can't hurt me with that thing."

He smacked the shotgun out of Colin's hands and moved to grab him by the neck. Colin ducked out of the way and took off running out the back door. The creature smashed through the back door and chased after him.

Colin didn't feel the sting of the Colorado spruce whipping across his cheek as he ducked into the woods. He was in his early thirties, and in decent shape, but he was also half-drunk and being chased by a monster from hell, so things weren't looking that good.

Because it was New Years Eve, Colin decided to start his resolution early and be bold for the first time in his life. He turned south and headed downhill toward Old Mill Creek. There was an abandoned mine there that he and his friends used to play around when they were kids. He remembered a passage there that he thought he might be able to double back and lose the monster.

The hill was much steeper than he had remembered from childhood. It was so steep that his desperate running turned more into some kind of flamboyant skipping.

"This is not how I want to die," Colin pleaded to himself.

All of a sudden there was a loud cracking noise and he was falling helplessly through the dark. Before he had time to react, he felt his left ankle snap like the fifty year old wooden planks he had broken through. Pain shot through his body like lightning. He screamed before he could stop himself from doing so. With no light there was no way of seeing how severe the break was. He could be bleeding out and not even know it. He had seen it with a cow once.

Growing up on the farm, he had been around animals his entire life and knew much of the mysteries of life and death. This is exactly what had happened with a six day old calf that had bled out throughout the night from a fractured leg. The bone had broken the skin after being stepped on by its much beefier mother. Colin was barely sixteen at the time and it was his job to herd the cattle back into the main pen before nightfall, but, like most barely-sixteen-year-olds, his attention span was lacking. He never noticed the irony of a baby calf's leg being trampled by its own mother. His father did, however, and never let him forget it.

Now here he sits with a broken ankle of his own waiting for death. Could this be some sort of karmic retribution? Is this fate?

He looked up. The moonlight lit up the dust as it fell

back into place in the hole above him. He could hear the desperate sounds of sniffs and pants. All of a sudden he heard voices above.

"BJ, what are you doing here? How did you get here?"

"I don't have much time, Chrissy. They're gonna know I snuck out soon. What the hell do you think you're doing?"

"Uhhh, well I am going to find this guy that I'm chasing and murder him. I'll probably choke him or stab him or beat him to death with a rock or a large branch or something. Why?"

"You can't do that!"

"Yes I can. I'm much much bigger than him. It would be very easy."

"No, I mean you're not allowed to do this. What do you think you're doing?!"

"I'm just following orders, man."

"You were ordered to kill my guy? What are the odds of that? Kind of coincidental, don't you think?"

"Your guy? This is who you were assigned to?"

"Yeah!"

"I didn't know that," Chrissy stopped to think for a moment, "but it's not like I have much of a choice, BJ."

"Yes, you do. We all have choices, Chrissy. If this has something to do with your vendetta against me then take it up with me right now. You're risking a lot by going this far. If you kill him, it changes everything."

"I didn't even know he was yours until now."

There was loud crashing noise and a flash of light in the sky.

"Oh no," BJ said as he looked around the sky, "I gotta split."

"Good. Bye," Chrissy said as he began walking

toward the broken planks Colin fell through.

"Chrissy, please. I'm begging you. Think this through," BJ pleaded.

"You hit me with a bus!"

"You hit ME with a bus!"

"You started it!"

"Look cat, I wish I could go back and change things. I really do."

"I don't," Chrissy said.

BJ was hurt by this. He turned to leave.

"We're still brothers," he said as he walked off into the night.

Colin listened as he heard his only chance of rescue leave. He was confused and terrified. He listened again, hoping for a clue as to where the monster was. There was silence. Maybe the creature had changed his mind after all. Maybe this BJ fella had talked some sense into the beast.

He began to crawl through the unlit corridor in front of him, begging himself not to scream with every painful movement. His ankle was definitely fractured. He could feel the warmth of the blood filling his boots. The pain sent him into the depths of despair, yet it was strangely invigorating. It was a reminder that he was still alive; that there was still a chance.

He moved through the narrow shafts at an impressive speed for such a condition. There was only darkness as he peered deeper into the tunnel. The cold was starting to soak in. He wasn't sure if he was shaking from the elements or from shock. Probably both he thought.

Why me? Colin couldn't figure out what he had done to deserve this. Nothing came to mind. He just didn't understand. He had done very little with his time on earth. He had lived a boring life. His greatest sin was having bad taste in phrasing.

"Fuck my face!" Colin screamed as the monster crashed down in front of him.

The monster looked at him with confusion.

"What did you say?" He thought maybe he heard that wrong.

"What do you want from me?!" Colin screamed. Snow was still drifting through the beams of moonlight cascading down the gaping hole above. As the creature slowly stood from the rubble, Colin got a good look at him for the first time. Demon from Hell?! The beast was easily eight feet tall and covered with black hair that stood as thick and sharp as a porcupine's quills. He was wearing an old, torn up pin-striped suit. The shirt had been ripped open exposing his chest. His eyes burned with an ancient madness, an incurable anger that could never be satisfied. He had hands that were perfectly manicured yet rough enough to sand off a layer of skin with one quick and easy pimp-slap. Had it not been for the long snarling snout and dagger like ears sticking above his head, cheating his true measurement, Colin would have thought that he looked more like a gorilla than a werewolf. Then again, of the two, he had less experience with a gorilla. In fact, he had none.

Colin forgot about his broken ankle as he tried to pivot and run away. The pain brought him to his back. He felt like a turtle on his shell. He was ashamed that he wasn't going to die standing up.

He watched as the creature started toward him, walking easily through the rubble and snow like they were as insignificant as grass. Oh my god, This is it! The creature stopped in front of him and picked up an old railway spike that used to tie down the rails for the mine carts.

    No words came to Colin's mind as the creature held the spike behind his head, eager to stab him with it. His life did not flash before his eyes like he assumed. He only saw Anna's face, and tried to remember her smell. He thought of a campfire. He remembered the first time he had met her. He remembered her laugh. Anna. He was at peace with his last thoughts; he loved her as deep as love could go.

    The creature stabbed him once through the heart. The young man took in as much air as he possibly could, then exhaled one last time; and as he stared into those furious eyes, Colin Lodestar fell softly into a place of quiet.

TWO

Of the three hundred and twenty-four Dukes of Hell, all but four of them hated dogs. That is because two of them actually were dogs; one of them had never had any experiences with dogs since a solid majority of them go to heaven; and one of them was very much blind and appreciated all that the species has done for his plight. This was the case for Amauros, the three hundred and twenty-fourth Duke of Hell.

Although Amauros couldn't see, blindness didn't slow him down much. He is a Duke of Hell after all, and it's pretty dark down there anyways; sight isn't really a big advantage. However, lately he had been spending quite a lot of time outside the gates of Hell and in the cubicles of purgatory, micromanaging the minions. As he strolled through the aisles, he could hear the sounds of demons hard at work, misdirecting the decency of man.

"Alright! Score! I just got one of my clients to take the batteries out of his grandmother's Life Alert® emergency response system and put them in the T.V. remote!" A demon cheered.

"Awesome job, Jared!" another demon shouted back. They always do this when he walks through. He usually tried to ignore them. He lifted the hood from his long cloak and put it over his head. Kissing ass never sat well with him, besides he was here for a different reason: he had a meeting.

He reached the end of the walkway and stepped into the elevator. His movements were so fluid that one would never guess him to be blind. As the elevator began to ascend, he thought back to his time as a lowly worker in the cubicles of purgatory. He was very good at his job. So good in fact that he had never actually spent time broiling in the wicked flares of Hell.

The logistics of purgatory were fairly simple. Everyone in the world is assigned to a demon or a "pusher." Said pusher then dedicates its existence in an effort to sway his or her client into sinful decisions; such as taking batteries out of grandma's Life Alert® system, or shaving the family bichon-frise. The possibilities are endless when it comes to poor decisions, and in this ever-changing planet there are more and more opportunities for a client to make them. Their motto: There's a sinner born every minute.

Amauros had many, many clients in his time, all of whose decisions he had a strong influence over and successfully lead them down the steady road south. It was his last client, however, that he had particular success with and which ultimately led to his promotion of Duke. When Old Scratch, himself, read the file on what Amauros had done with a certain German named Adolf, he was so moved by Amauros' efforts that he felt his talent was wasted in purgatory; he was meant for bigger things. He was immediately promoted to the three hundred and twenty fourth Duke of Hell and given control over thirteen legions.

The demons loved working in purgatory. With every

soul they help condemn to Hell, they get another stint in purgatory. It may seem like a dead-end job, literally, but it definitely beats crisping in the eternal toasters of Hell.

The elevator reached the 600th floor with a cheeky ding as the doors opened to his penthouse office. Amauros strolled out of the elevator and into his office. He could smell the cologne covered musk that shrouded Chrissy over in front of the salt water fish tank. Amouros couldn't watch the fish swimming, himself, but he enjoyed knowing that they were there. It was a power thing.

"Lodestar is dead," Chrissy said.

"Good work, Chrissy. That was an important job"

"I stabbed him with a railway spike."

"Cool," Amauros said.

"So... I guess this means... I can go back to my cubicle?"

"Oh, no. No, not at all. We have too much to do now. This is just the beginning," Amauros said, "This is my destiny."

Ever since his death, Chrissy had worked closely with Amauros. He was crucial to his plan; however, he wouldn't have known it. Life in Purgatory isn't easy. If Amauros could have felt any kind of affection he would surely have felt it for the poor guy. Feelings and friendship, however, do not last in Purgatory. They slowly fade away much like everything else, even one's appearance changes after time in the Purg. You become a shadow of your former self. A monster. It's all part of the whole 'eternal suffering' thing.

"Did you know that that the Lodestar guy, was my brother's client?"

"Chrissy," Amauros sat down behind his desk, "I didn't want you to be distracted. I know what your

brother did to you. You got a bum deal, being sent down here. I didn't want it to cloud your judgment."
Chrissy sat quietly.

"You did a great job! At any rate the first part of the plan is in action. All we have to do now is wait. My math is somewhere around 28 years, 3 months, and 16 days."

"How do you know he won't just go to heaven? Maybe they'll pull some strings or something since we broke the rules."

"Because I know how those pious bastards work. They won't break the rules because they can't and besides that, Chrissy," Amauros turned around and locked his barren eyes straight into the demon's. "I'll soon have a man on the inside."

"Who's that?" Chrissy asked.

"You."

THREE

Colin opened his eyes to black. It was sweltering hot and he could hear what he only imagined as an evil clown snickering in the darkness. There was a strange feeling washing over him. He felt lighter, yet almost more solid. Healthy. He wasn't breathing, and couldn't find it in himself to remember how to.

"Welcome to Hell, bitch!" someone screamed. It sounded like the lead singer from some eighties hair metal band. The kind of music Colin never bothered with. Because it sucks.

Colin whimpered, "Oh, God no!"

The lights flickered on and Colin found himself lying on his back staring into the black-rimmed glasses of the most awkward looking thirty-something year old that he could have imagined. There was a small group of people laughing from the hilarious joke that Colin was obviously not a part of.

"Don't worry," Black-Rimmed Glasses laughed as he helped Colin to his feet. "We're just kidding around with you. You're not in Hell, but you are definitely dead."

Colin was speechless. You can't do that can you? Joking around with someone about their soul burning forever in the scariest place of all human imagination is just downright mean

He watched Black-Rimmed Glasses walk over to the

air conditioner and reach up to turn it back on.

"I do this to a lot of the new guys here. It's a funny joke, right?"

"Not really," Colin said as he looked around. He was still on edge.

He looked around. They were in a small room with only a couch near the back wall. Layers of bubble wrap lined the walls.

"What's with all the bubble wrap?" Colin asked.

"That? Oh, some people hit this room harder than others. Usually if they were in an explosion or something like that," Glasses said.

"So is this Heaven?" Colin asked.

"Heaven? What?? Slow down kid," Glasses said, "You're not in Heaven. Not yet, anyway. You're in the in-between. You're in Limbo! The Rocky Mountain Division. It's awesome here!"

"Limbo… Okay… This is not what I would have expected. What a shit day."

"Could be worse," Glasses shrugged.

"How?!"

"I don't know… You could have ended up in a Walmart or something. Oh! What if the afterlife was just a big, long musical?"

"I like musicals," Colin said.

"Yeah, so do I," Glasses said, "But an eternal musical?"

"That's a good point."

"Oh right! I'm Brad, by the way. You probably want to know what is going on. I'll show you to the orientation room."

He walked past Colin and held the door open for him. He could see on the other side of it a large white sign with golden letters spelling: Arrivals.

"This way, buddy," Brad said.

      *   *   *   *   *

The orientation room was filled with the furious chatter of computer keyboards, a glorious orchestra of nerds. There seemed to be at least two hundred confused souls in there hoping for an answer; each one of them searching on the computers in front of them. It was laid out like a massive high-school library, with tables and chairs scattered throughout. A large window filled the far side wall and let in a perfect sunshine. As Brad led Colin through the symphony he noticed that they all seemed to be about the same age as him. All of them: young women and men who were cheated on a long and lasting life at the hands of a callous and unsympathetic world. He wondered how many of them had been stabbed by a demon-wolf-gorilla in a pin-striped suit.

"Here we go," Brad said, as they approached an empty desk. There was an easy breeze coming from somewhere above them.

"Have a seat here and just log in with this temporary user ID and password," he said as he handed him a little strip of paper, "From there you just need to check your new messages and there should be a welcome note explaining everything. We used to have paper pamphlets for all of this," he rolled his eyes, "but Jesus is kind of a tree hugger. So we went green in '81."

Colin had never actually seen a computer before. His family didn't have the money or need for a one. He was amazed by it. The black and green screen was incredibly vivid. He had a tough time with the keyboard though, being that none of the letters were in order. You would have thought that the scientists would have got this part right. He aimed his index finger directly at the down-arrow key and began to peck at it like a chicken pecks at corn. He scrolled down until the highlighter bar was in position to type in his login ID. He looked down at the strip of paper in his hand. It read:

Login ID: Lodestar
Password: 8

Colin couldn't help but feel that this use of paper went against the "go green" mentality that Jesus was trying to implement. He typed in the info.

The computer whizzed to life as the screen began to scroll downwards, reading what could only be deciphered as some sort of secret nerd language; a language that relies heavily on capital "C's" and colons. All of a sudden the screen stopped and read:

<New Messages-Click Return>

He searched the keys for the return button and pushed it.

Why is the return button also the enter button? If you entered aren't you already there? How could you return?

The message appeared.

<Welcome to orientation! We hope that this message finds you in good spirits. LOL :) You probably have a lot of questions. We hope to answer most of these; however, any remaining questions can be answered by your supervisor after you have read this.>

<Introduction: Limbo was built thousands of years ago. It operates as a catalyst for good decisions. Our workers are each assigned one soul on Earth. It is the Watcher's responsibility (you) to encourage them to do right. Remember, there are forces out there that are constantly trying to sway these souls into darkness, so don't be shy. If you fill your judgment quota and successfully help lead your soul through a long and virtuous life, then you will have earned your ticket to paradise! If, however, for some reason your assignment meets an early demise and no judgment can be implemented, then you will be replaced and sent to the waiting room. Don't panic! You will still go to heaven! It will just take a little longer. There you will be given a number and will wait until your number is called. The current approximate wait time is: 28 years 3 months 16 days.>

Colin thought of the poor soul whom he had replaced and sent to that very room now. They are probably last in line, he thought.

<Judgment Quota: Everyone has the opportunity to a live a long and happy life. People are faced with decisions every day which impact that opportunity in a positive or negative way. Every decision has a consequence. However, due to the high volumes of choices being made every day, our judgment panel has their hands full. Therefore, we have implemented a more convenient and leaner system of deciding the eternal fate of each soul. We have set up five random choices, or tests, throughout everyone's life. These tests are totally random and completely confidential; and will ultimately decide whether or not one goes to heaven or hell. You will never know when your client is being judged, so treat every moment as if it were the test of a lifetime, because it just might be.

Each test will allow our panels to judge your client on five different values. These values are:

Compassion
Honor
Truth
Modesty
Being Cool

Pass these (well, at least three out of five ;) and both you, and the soul you rode in on, will have earned a ticket to Heaven. We're excited to have you on board! Feel free to ask your supervisor any other questions you may have. Be Good!>

<End of Session>

Colin was still burning with questions about his death. He didn't have the energy for more about his afterlife. Still, he couldn't help but wonder about this "client" he was going to be assigned. I wonder what they'll be like, he thought. He felt like a giddy little nine year old again and getting his first pen pal.

A green light flashed on above his terminal and before he could say "Jesus H. Christ in holy tights" he was led out of the room by a woman in white.

"Hi, I'm Leah. I'm your supervisor. Let's get you to your quarters and get you set up. There should be some wine delivered to you soon. A little house warming present," She smiled.

She led him down a skywalk and he had a chance to look out the window. It was breathtaking. Limbo looked like a bunch of different airports all connected by golden roads. He could see light peaking through the clouds above. There were glowing green fields in the distance with what seemed to look like caves. Incredible.

"Limbo was built thousands and thousands of years ago. There are some people who think that it was built because of a challenge from Satan. No one knows for sure. We just know enough to do our jobs," Leah explained.

"This is a lot to take in at once," Colin admitted.

"The wine helps," Leah said.

As they approached the door to his room, she unlocked it and gave him the key. He stepped through the door and instantly felt at home. His quarters were cozy and well-lit from a huge window looking out over the fields. There were different screens around the room, and in the far corner was a desk with a leather chair and what looked like a crystal ball. A small kitchen was to his right with a walk in closet full of wine. Suddenly he wasn't so worried, which was rare for Colin. Incredible.

"Welcome to your new home," Leah said as she walked back down the hall.

"Wait... I still have some questions! What about the person I'm supposed to watch? How does any of this work?"

"The paper work is on your desk. Your client has just been born. His name is Jack. You have plenty of time, don't worry. How much trouble can a little baby be?"

FOUR

Twenty-eight years later...

Somewhere out on Highway 160, just a few miles passed South Fork, Colorado, you could take a deep breath, close your eyes, and listen beyond the serenity of the Rio Grande National Forest and barely make out the faint sounds of absolute terror emanating from a brand new, used, 1998 blue Ford Econoline.

The conversion van was plummeting down the highway at an increasingly dangerous speed. Every now and then, a wheel breaking its grip from the road as it struggled to hold on, keeping it from hurtling over the edge and joining the graveyard of muscle cars and station wagons below. Each of them too precariously fixed to tow out, lost to the appetite of the mountains.

The screams inside the vehicle were all directed toward the driver's seat, where Jack Charlton was fast asleep.

Jack was dreaming. He was dreaming of glory and power. He was dreaming of space and magic. He was dreaming of women.

He was dreaming that he was in an airport. It was alive with folks of different banners, coming and going. The stale air was cold against his naked chest. He kept losing a tooth.

"You're all set to board the plane now, sir." The attendant said, as she scanned his ticket.

"Where am I going?" he asked.

She directed him down the line and he boarded the plane. Another flight attendant greeted him on the plane.

"Welcome aboard Mr. Charlton, but I have some bad news. It seems that you are the only one booked in first class today. It looks like it's just you and the four of us hot, horny flight attendants."

"But where are we going?" he asked.

One of them grabbed him by his shoulders and slammed him down in his seat.

"Easy ladies," he winced, "my dangling sailor likes a little cushion when he arrives to port."

He leaned back and looked out the window, ignoring the women as they bent down to help each other take his pants off. That's when he heard the screams. They were distant and vague, sounding like what one could only describe as screams of absolute terror. He looked down to the ladies. They were gone, vanished. He heard the screams again.

"Make up to gum other duck ert!"

Germans?

He looked around only to see that he was completely alone; all except for a strange dog sitting in the chair besides him. He thought it was a labradoodle. He, however, had smoked quite a lot of weed in his twenty eight years, and wasn't entirely sure he even knew what a labradoodle was.

"Designer breed," one of the stewardesses explained.

Jack looked at her, and then back to the dog.

"Wake up you dumb motherfucker," the labradoodle said.

"Are you German?" he asked.

"WAKE UP YOU DUMB MOTHERFUCKER!"

Jack opened his eyes to find himself behind the wheel of the van. The screams from the passengers blended in with the screeches from the exterior of the van against the metal guard rails on the side of the highway. As the van flew through the darkness Jack sprang to action. He gripped the steering wheel and slowly brought the van back into his lane, careful not to overcorrect and send them into a spin, plummeting down the side of the mountain.

"Jesus Christ!!" Their drummer, Matt, screamed from the passenger seat.

"What? What's wrong?" Jack said.

"What's wrong? You almost killed us! You fell asleep at the wheel of the goddamn car!"

"It's a conversion van."

"Huh?"

"It's a conversion van, not a car."

"You fell asleep at the wheel of the goddamn conversion van!"

"Oh, relax. I was barely asleep. It's all good, man."

"Barely asleep!?"

"Yeah. I had the weirdest dream."

"Unbelievable," Their fiddler, Dave, said from the back.

"Yeah, it was. There was a labradoodle that spoke German."

"Designer breeds," their bassist, Adam, said.

"That's exactly what the flight attendant said!"

Matt slapped him in the back of the head.

"Hey!" Jack said, "I'm driving here!"

A few moments of silence passed. The van was filled with a quiet that could only be measured by the previous chaos. It was uncomfortable and Jack felt that his band mates already thought of him as kind of a dumbass. Why bring it back up by apologizing? If you're living in the past then you have no future; or something like that. Besides, they still had hours to go and plenty of time to gain redemption. They were planning on driving through the night for a gig they had the next afternoon.

The Devil Wears Nada was used to overnight journeys through perilous terrains. For the past few years they have been spending an average of two hundred and ninety days a year on the road. It was a brutal circuit filled with seedy bars and ski resorts, cheap drinks and free drugs. However, after years of disparaging work and long days, they were well on their way of becoming one of the biggest acts in the Rocky Mountains. Soon they could quit their daytime restaurant jobs. Soon they would be delivered.

Jack had no real reason to be tired. He had slept most of the day and a good part of the night, and he had only been driving for thirty minutes. I can do this. This is nothing to me. I once smoked an entire joint underwater. This is easy. I'm a pro.

Far away in the distant afterlife, 28 short years after his death, Colin Lodestar was the only one who noticed Matt smack him in the head as Jack almost drifted back asleep again.

FIVE

Back in 1953, Chicago was alive and well, and you could find its heart and soul at The Green Hill Jazz Club. The Green Hill was one of most popular jazz clubs around. Acts from all around the country would embrace their instruments on that delicate stage with a sovereign pride. It was as if they were grasping a shining brass scepter of groove.

The Twins played there on the first Thursday of every month, and people would herd into the club like a bunch of funky sheep. The dance floor was filled with hep cats and jive turkeys from many different beginnings. But on this particular Thursday night, there was an especially mean rug being cut.

The Twins were a four piece jazz band fronted by a well dressed black man on a baby grand piano. He was a short and stocky man in a smart pinstriped suit. Silver-rimmed sunglasses covered his eyes while sweat reflected from the stage lights above.

The sounds painted the air with gentle blues and nostalgic greens. A hazy smell of reefer blended with the salty sweat that seemed to stick to your very skin. As the bartender lit a smoke, the band finished up a rendition of "Seven Steps to Heaven." The easy summer breeze was cool to the touch as it meandered through the stage door in the back. The room felt like sex and paradise.

The crash of the cymbals rang through the night as the song came to an end.

Another stocky black man in a pinstriped suit put down his trumpet and approached the microphone.

"Everyone just stay smooth, we're gonna take a short break and we'll be back in no time at all."

He put his trumpet down and walked off stage. Looking back behind him, he saw his twin brother, BJ, standing from his piano to approach a group of beautiful women. He shook his head in frustration and turned around to talk to his brother. As he approached the small crowd, BJ was obviously ignoring him.

"BJ, come outside with us. We need to talk about the next set!"

"I'm a little busy here, Chrissy. Don't worry though; I think I know what I'm doing. You're the one that needs to worry about the next set. You sound like a dying seal that's being raped by an angry dinosaur up there."

This enraged Chrissy.

"Juicy, get your black ass outside before I walk." He meant it.

BJ watched as his brother turned around and stormed his way through the crowd. He looked back at the gaggle of women.

"It's probably just the hemorrhoids. You know trumpet players…always straining." And with a wink and a smile he turned to follow his brother outside.

The alley was eerily quiet in comparison to the noise from inside the club. The breeze was cool against BJ's perspiring skin. They could smell the Chicago River from a few blocks away. He half heartedly looked up and down the alley for his brother. The sounds of traffic grew louder as he approached the end. The traffic was busier than usual for this time of night. This momentarily distracted BJ in his search, and his brother's voice from his side startled him.

"What's it going to take, BJ?"

Chrissy was sitting against the brick building next to a dumpster. A cigarette lit. He resembled a broken derelict, a brother forsaken. The streetlights showed the age of his suit. The weight of the world was heavy on his mind.

BJ wasn't sure how to respond.

"What do you mean?" he said.

"What is going to take for you to give me the respect I deserve? It's no secret that you have always been the one with the talent. I get it. This stuff has always been easy for you. And, honestly, that isn't really what even bothers me." He stood from the wall and approached his brother. "What bothers me is that I have worked harder than you at everything only to get just so close to the standard you set. I have always had the drive. I book the shows. I handle the money. I handle the band. What do you do?! You make a mockery of me! You treat me like shit and smoke reefer all day! And when I ask you to do one thing you…"

"Chrissy, you're my brother and I love you, but face the facts. Without me you don't have a band. You can book all you want with you and the three black musketeers in there, but without me you're just another busted jazz ensemble playing another busted version of Greensleeves." BJ grabbed the cigarette from his brother's hand and took a drag. Chrissy stared back at him, his eyes blackened with anger. "So what's it going to take, Chrissy? I'll tell you what it's going to take. It's going to take you chilling the fuck out and stop getting bent out of shape about every little fucking thing I do. The sooner you accept your role and quit trying to steal a little piece of my spotlight, the sooner we'll both be happy with the way things are going. You're right, you'll never be at my level, so quit trying. Just keep booking the shows, keep counting the goddamned money, and keep that jealous little soup cooler of yours shut. Be thankful that you have a player of my caliber in this fucking group, because if you weren't my brother, you would have been walking a long time ago."

There was a long silence as BJ dropped his smoke and put it out with his shoe. He turned to walk back toward the club. Rage burned into Chrissy like a branding iron into a bull. The world went red. It was the kind of anger that leaves a scar. He lost control and barreled into the back of his twin brother. The two of them hit the ground rolling, but Chrissy was back on his feet quickly. He began to kick his brother in the ribs as he was trying to stand up.

"Chrissy, stop!" BJ gasped.

Chrissy took a moment to think, but the rage had consumed him. He looked down at his brother as he was on all fours trying to catch his breath. The thoughts of those cheesy piano licks coming from his brother were just fuel to the fire. He let out a deep groan, and with one fell stomp he crushed his brother's hand; the very hand that had always put BJ a step above Chrissy in everyone's eyes. BJ screamed and grasped his hand as he rolled onto his side. Chrissy stood back.

BJ laid in the fetal position holding his broken hand to his chest. There was a moment of silence before BJ spoke.

"Chrissy, I'm sorry. I never meant to hurt you, I'm just

jealous. I've never had the motivation that you have. I never had the drive. This isn't easy for me either, you know. No one respects me."

The twin brother's eyes softened. He began to feel dreadfully sorry for attacking his brother. He approached BJ to help him up. As he leaned toward his brother, a deep scraping pain shot through his face. BJ had hit him with a piece of concrete hidden behind his back. He could taste the blood in his mouth. Chrissy charged again.

They tumbled out of the alley toward the busy street. The scrap came to a pause as Chrissy held a battered BJ by the collar of his shirt.

"You have never treated me like a brother!" he screamed. "You never cared!"

He looked up the street to see a bus speeding toward them.

"I hate you, BJ. I have hated you for as long as I can remember," Chrissy continued.

BJ could see the darkness sweeping over Chrissy as he decided to kill him right then and there. Everything seemed to slow down as BJ felt his brother shift his momentum to throw him into the oncoming bus. He grabbed Chrissy's belt as he began to fall into the street. Chrissy was caught off balance and rolled over top of his brother, both of them in front of the bus. The honk seemed distant and muffled as they both looked up and realized their fate. The screech of the tires and the crunch of the bones made the entire block stand still. The twins were dead before they felt the bus hit. One was going to Heaven. One was going to Hell.

SIX

Jack was eight minutes late to work. He was shirtless and driving his van northbound on I-25. The heat was exaggerated in the stop and go traffic. There was a cigarette burning out in the left hand as he changed the radio station with his right.

Milt is going to kill me. Showing up eight minutes late to work was certainly not the worst thing that Jack had done, but it wasn't helping his cause.

Pepper's Bar and Grill was the paradigm of corporate hospitality. There was a spec for everything. The salt and peppers need to be at least 90 percent full. You have a very specific birthday song to sing. You greet your table within two minutes and you offer one alcoholic drink and one non alcoholic drink. You check back after "two bites" or two minutes and make sure that their micro waved steak is up to standards. You drop the check with your name written on it and a clever "thanks" and for goodness sake you don't accidentally make racist remarks toward the Asian guests. Just because you have an Oriental Salad on the menu doesn't mean that every person with an Asian background is going to order it. They like burgers, too.

When Jack was 19, he started out as a host. He would stand at the foyer and greet every person who walked through with a smile and an open door. He was a natural. At the root, Jack was a genuinely happy person. He loved life and he loved people and he loved to spread joy with a smile and an inspiring quip. If you were feeling low, he would bring you up. Maybe not in the healthiest of ways, but he would bring you up however he could.

The management recognized his joyful disposition and immediately upgraded him to a server position. Jack soared as a waiter. He loved the fast pace and thrived off of the sense of community he shared with his fellow coworkers. To him, there were few things less entertaining than the abstract bitterness that one achieves after years of waiting tables.

Approach table.

"Hello folks, how are you doing today?"

"Coffee," the patron would interrupt.

"One coffee coming right up," the server would say, cheerfully.

Walk away from table and into the kitchen.

"Oh you're doing 'coffee' today?! Oh you're feeling 'coffee?!' Well that's fucking great. Me? Oh thanks for asking. I'm feeling real fucking 'iced tea!' " they would rant as they would prepare a coffee. Any other servers in the kitchen would nod in agreement. That table sucked. Those people suck.

The "back of the house" was always full of rage and passive aggression. You could just walk back and listen to the chatter and learn something about life.

"It's not a 'diet' soda after six refills, fat ass!"

"These pieces of shit high schoolers DO NOT all have the same birthday…"

"IDIOTS! Your burger isn't cheaper because you

asked for no onions!"

There is a certain wisdom one can acquire from a stint in the service industry: people are pigs, people are liars, and people are cheap.

Jack, however, refused to fall victim to the negativity. He focused on the good in the world. He paid no mind to the grumps that would sit in his section; instead he would laugh with the kind families and give balloons to the kids. His joy was as infectious as a cold, and sometimes just as annoying, too.

It was this attitude that kept him climbing the ladder. After a little over a year of serving tables, he was trained as a Pepper's Bar and Grill bartender. Jack was happy with this gig. He was meeting new people and making great money. As the years passed and his music slowly built, this would be the perfect day job.

Eventually, he found little games he would play with himself or his coworkers that would serve to keep himself entertained throughout the shifts. He loved to try and slip ice cubes into the other server's aprons. Sometimes he would try different accents at his tables. He liked to replace the word "folks" with "fucks" and see if anyone noticed.

"And here's the check. You fucks have a nice day, now."

Jack loved his job. It wasn't until his breakup with Olivia that he started slipping.

He parked his blue conversion van in the parking lot like it was a hatchback. The tires screeched, and before the echo could dissipate from the parking lot, Jack was out the door and heading toward the job. He had his apron already tied on, and he was fighting his way through his black polo shirt as he reached the door. Milt was waiting.

"Jack," Milt said in a calm collected voice, "you're late again. You were late the last two shifts. Everything okay?"

"Yeah man. Everything is cool. I just had a late gig last night. I'm sorry, man."

"Okay, well Jorge got your bar setup for you. We have a big 'to go' order to get ready by the time we're open. Apparently, these fuckers control time now. They decide when we open."

The plight of a servant knew no hierarchy in the restaurant biz.

Jack took advantage of his unexpected five extra minutes and went out by the dumpsters to smoke a joint.

*   *   *   *   *

"You should really get your client to quit doing so many drugs so often, Colin." Brad, Colin's first acquaintance and neighbor from down the hall, said.

"Well, Brad, I've been so preoccupied with trying to get him to give up the hookers that I've kind of put the drug thing on hold for a bit."

Brad stared through his black glasses, hesitant to laugh. Over the years, the two had become friends, but he still wasn't quite sure how to handle Colin. Irony is wasted in Limbo.

Colin explained, "Look, I was kidding, but I'm not sure what to do about it. I mean, the drugs have, weirdly enough, kept Jack out of more trouble than they've gotten him into. I mean, the guy has been so stoned that he has actually missed out on a lot of opportunities to do some major damage." He continued, "And not only that, but they've kept him from getting hurt, too. You remember that time I was telling you about when he got so stoned that he forgot to go pick his brother up from the airport? Well, turns out that his drummer, Matt, went in his place and got mugged by a homeless guy named Pinkerton! He got stabbed in the stomach with a toothbrush! I mean have you ever even heard of that happening outside of a prison!? So in a weird way, drugs have kind of protected Jack from himself and the world around him. It's like a trippy, little protective bubble." Colin held his hand to his chin. "That reminds me! I need to apologize to Daryl for getting his client stabbed."

"Hey, it's your time and he's your client. I'm just saying that I've seen how these things end up. Trust me, these drugs are going to catch up, and when they do, it's going to be in a big way, brother." Brad concluded, "Trust me."

He walked out of Colin's room.

Colin walked over to his desk, rotated what seemed to be a glass ball, and began to look into it. The Watchers had many different ways of watching over their client, but the gazing ball was Colin's favorite.

It had been 28 years in Limbo and he had spent every single day of it watching over Jack Charlton, from the moment he was born.

From birth on it could be said that Jack's mom and dad were either unsung parental geniuses, or they were weird as shit. Either way, Jack's upbringing was far from the norm. At the age of eight, while other kids were riding bikes and building forts; Jack was able to identify twelve different types of tires from their skid marks and could sketch people's faces from memory.

Jack grew up in a little town just south of the Denver Metro. His father had a mysterious career at Lowry Air Force base in Littleton and traveled quite often, usually to a small town in Nevada. His mother ran an organic food shop and liked to decorate random items with buttons. It was a strange childhood, but easier than many. His folks were both well to do, and he never went without, but Jack always felt that there was something bigger out there. He knew that not everyone catches their star, but he was bound and determined to catch his.

Jack loved music as a kid, but was never any good at it. He went through three piano instructors before he had finished the 4th grade. To be fair, it wasn't just his poor playing, but his stubborn attitude and the fact that he may have accidentally been the catalyst in the death of one of the instructor's cats. How was Jack to know that the neighbors raised jackals? But, easy come easy go, and Jack's mother finally gave up on any kind of instruction for him. However, with all of what would seem to be obstacles to the everyman, Jack powered through. He laughed in the face of failure, sneered at oppression, and scoffed at the hands of conformity. He loved music and the free world so much that it was only natural that his folks eventually found taking these things from him as the only effective source of discipline.

At the age of 16, Jack had begun to write his own music out of necessity. He had neglected to do his chores and his father had taken the steps to discipline him in the only way he knew. He had taken the speakers out of his car, removed his stereo from his room, taken away the speakers from the computer, and removed all headphones from the house. His father never did have the heart to take away his son's guitar, though, and it was from times like these that Jack learned to create. He would emulate his favorite musicians and try to rewrite their songs from scratch. After a while, Jack began to feel like he was always on the wrong side of the speakers. It was his music that needed to be played out. He wanted to inspire people.

All people's lives can be measured in chapters, and at the age of 20, Jack decided to start a new one. He packed his things and headed to the city in search of others who would join his cause. Jack eventually put together The Devil Wears Nada, and they began to start a small following. And since the day he was born, Colin Lodestar had been watching over him and trying his damnedest to keep him on the path of good.

As he watched him grow through the years, Colin grew to love Jack much like a brother. He took great care to help him make the right decisions whenever he could, and because he never knew when Jack was being tested, every decision that he made seemed much more stressful. He often wondered if Purgatory's pusher assigned to Jack felt any bond toward him as well. He certainly had feelings for him. His pusher hated Jack, but he hated Colin Lodestar even more.

SEVEN

Every little piece of the world is connected. A drop of rain falls on the fluttering wings of a butterfly in Tiananmen Square causing a heat wave in Spain that causes a family to move to Canada and open a poutine restaurant that causes an orange-skinned, billionaire demagogue to lead the free world. It is cause and effect on a string, and through a shimmering spiral of time and space, coincidence and desire, money and sex: everything is possible. Everything has a loophole. This rings true in the afterlife as well. Everything has a meaning to someone, and sometimes the smallest thing can turn into the perfect solution. This is the case for Amauros.

In 1915, the tiniest cluster of cells split off resulting into two tiny identical zygotes, which grew into two tiny identical babies, who grew into two identical jazz musicians, who then beat each other up after a gig and rolled into a bus, which caused two identical deaths. Some would call that the circle of life. Amauros called it a jackpot.

Chrissy had been Amauros' left and right hands since he arrived in Purgatory. He did his laundry. He took care of his landscaping. He helped with the day to day activities in The Purg. Most importantly, though, he was the ticket into Limbo. When Chrissy and BJ died, it was Chrissy who was in the wrong, and it was BJ who was protecting himself. Whether BJ had instigated the whole thing or not doesn't matter. That is what set each twin on their path into the afterlife. In regard to twins, even though the soul may not be a match, looks still are.

This was Amauros' ticket to Heaven.

*   *   *   *   *

It was just another average, run of the mill, garden variety, dime-a-dozen, humdrum, so-so, middle of the road, boring ass morning at the Rocky Mountain Division of Limbo. Brad was relaxing on Colin's couch. His Watcher's quarters was in the middle of a spirited fumigation. Yes, bugs have souls, too. He was working remotely and staying with Colin for a couple days. Colin didn't mind. He had never had a roommate back on Earth.

Earth. Even though he had been in Limbo for nearly as long as he was alive, it still felt strange to think that he was on a different realm now. He no longer lived on Earth. He was a resident of Limbo now, and until he brought Jack in as sin free as possible, he wasn't going anywhere.

"Know what would be cool, man?" Brad asked rhetorically. "Is if we could just have died and went to Heaven! This blows some serious golden trumpets. I mean come on! Gary has been at home sick for days now. All he does is watch TV or sit on the shitter. Sometimes he does both! I'm going insane." He looked up from the couch toward Colin. "Let's switch for a bit. Jack may be a lazy stoner, but at least he tends to get into some crazy situations."

"Jack is a major pain in the ass! Are you kidding?!" Colin rebutted. "I can't take my eyes off of him for any longer than five minutes, or he's trying to sleep with anything that moves! He's an animal. If I wasn't here, who knows what his pusher would be getting him to do!"

Colin continued, "I'm telling ya, man. I don't sleep at night. I have trouble eating. I always thought that the silver lining of dying young would be keeping my youth in eternity, but I honestly think that I'm getting gray hairs! This dude is aging me. I'm drinking a few bottles of wine a night these days." He sighed. "Olivia really did a number on him. I wish he was still with her. She kept him in line better than I ever could."

"Speaking of wine," Brad said as he stood up and headed toward the kitchen. At that moment they heard the alarms.

EIGHT

They were standing in the darkened halls of The Rocky Mountain Division of Limbo, just outside Colin's room. The alarms were ringing for a good fifteen minutes, but then everything was shut off. The lights, the Watchers' equipment, everything was turned off together. It was too quiet.

"What the hell is the protocol on this one?" Colin asked. "I remember some kind of training on this, but that was during my orientation twenty something years ago."

"Well, if the alarms stopped, then I guess it's over." Brad continued, "Maybe we should head to the orientation room or something?"

"Well, we're not going to figure anything out just standing here. Let's go," Colin said firmly. They began down the hall.

"Where is everyone else?" Brad asked.

"They're probably already in the orientation room. Or, here's a guess, they haven't been drinking wine for the last thirty years and remembered something we don't."

They made their way to a covered skywalk that

connected the Watchers' quarters to the rest of the Rocky Mountain Division. They stopped to look out the windows and view the rest of Limbo. The usually well lit airport-like buildings were dark. Each gigantic concourse that connected the different division looked abandoned.

"Wow. The whole place is dark. What is going on?" Brad said

"Look!" Colin interrupted.

They peered down below and saw them. There were thousands of demons making their way down the fields and toward their building. Smoke was rising in the distance. There wasn't a single resident of Limbo in sight.

"It's an attack!"

There hadn't been an attack on Limbo in hundreds of years, and the attacks that did happen have never been successful. The angels were in charge of security. An army of God is something not to be trifled with. It's almost as if the attacks just happened as a reminder that the other side was still there. It was more of an annoyance than anything else. The demons of Purgatory were a bunch of punks, sometimes.

Colin noticed a strange figure making his way through the middle of the battalion. The figure was at least two heads taller than any other creature down there. Colin recognized the way it moved. He froze as he remembered the eyes. He could almost hear its breathing in his head. He knew exactly who it was and if he was still alive his heart would have stopped. It was Chrissy. It was the creature that killed him.

Just then a flash of light surged through the sky, and the angels were on the demons before they could react. The angels did not use weapons. They only did what was needed to restrain the demons and carry them out of the city. The term 'army' was a stretch. They seemed more like a sort of peace loving, gang of eagles as they flew through the air and plucked demons from the ground. Colin watched as one of them shoved a flower up a demons ass before drop kicking him into the sky. A flash of light broke as the demon disappeared. Okay, so maybe not all of them were as gentle as the others.

Just then Colin looked back toward the monster only to find that he was gone.

"Where did he go?!" he asked, with a hint of panic on his breath.

"Who?" Brad half heartedly responded.

"The big gorilla looking thing that was leading the attack, I just saw him, and now he's gone."

"I didn't see anyone like that. Maybe the angels kicked it out?"

Colin wanted to believe that, but he knew deep down inside that this wouldn't be that easy. He was shocked. He never would have guessed that he would ever see that creature again. His mind went back to that cold December night; back to the night he was killed. Something wasn't right with all of this. Then, Colin remembered something.

He remembered the voices he heard as he was hiding in the mine. He remembered something that the other voice said. *I'm just looking out for my guy down there.* Colin realized that he had to find his Watcher. He would have an answer.

"Come on. We have to go right now," Colin said as he grabbed Brad by the shoulders and pulled him away from the windows. "We have to get to the waiting room."

"The waiting room? That's the last place we should go! That's the only entrance to Heaven. Where do you think these demons are heading? Starbucks?! They've got more of those in Hell than we have here. I can promise that,"

Brad said.

"The creature I was talking about, the one that I saw. That's the same thing that killed me. I remembered right before I died though, that there were voices. Someone came down and tried to stop him from killing me. I think it was my Watcher. The weird thing, though, is that they knew each other. They had history together, Brad. And now that freaking demon dude is here? That's no coincidence. I think my Watcher will know what's going on."

They ran down the hall to the first elevator they found. Brad pushed the button for the top floor.

"Okay, well how do you even know who your Watcher is? How are we even gonna find him in there? You haven't been in the waiting room before. The word 'room' isn't exactly accurate. The place is more like a bazaar or something. It's huge."

"I'm not sure," Colin said. "Maybe he'll recognize me. I remember his name was 'Juice' and the other demon's name is 'Chrissy'"

"Juice and Chrissy? Totally normal," Brad commented as he pushed the elevator button. "Going up."

*   *   *   *   *

Outside in the grounds of Limbo, the battle came to a halt. The angels were finishing up tossing out any straggler demon they found, and were beginning to head back toward the light in the sky. All seemed to be back to normal. Except for a rustling in some bushes near the dumpsters toward the back entrance of the Rocky Mountain Division.

The Watchers of Limbo were people of the world once, as well. And just because they no longer had to breathe or needed food and water, didn't mean that they didn't like snacks and the occasional glass of wine. Souls still have hobbies and like to have fun. They form friendships and need quiet time just like any of us. In a way, the souls of Limbo were much more human than the people of Earth. There was no social media to bog them down; no psychological warfare on the masses in the name of consumerism. There were no Kardashians to keep up with. The only major difference was the souls of Limbo didn't need all the logistical bodily function stuff; most likely because they were all dead as shit.

Limbo was very much like a city of incredibly large airports or train stations. There were thousands of different concourses and divisions spread around, each in charge of different regions of the world. There was the Eastern America Division, The Texas Division, and The California Division, and so on and so on. Vegas had its own building, which was always getting audited. Then there were the different sections for the other countries, each with their own Divisions. The world is a big place, and Limbo was, too. The infrastructure was very similar to large cities as well. There were roads and bridges, and different buildings with other functions besides just watching over the people on earth. This was to be used to Chrissy's advantage.

At the back of the Rocky Mountain Division were a number of large garage doors. Next to the doors were a number of dumpsters. Next to the dumpsters were a number of bushes. Behind the bushes hid Chrissy and his crackerjack eight man team of demons, waiting for their moment.

"Okay, so listen up, you scoundrels," Chrissy gathered his crew around him and began reading a piece of paper. "'In about 20 minutes, the wine delivery truck is going to show up. Hijack the truck, and use it to sneak into the building. Once inside, get into the dumbwaiter and take it up to the 45th floor. Sneak through the orientation room and into the waiting room where, after finding your idiot brother, have your team bring him down to the boiler room and keep him locked up and hidden. Then take his place in the waiting room. No one will even know he's missing. Then we wait for me to make my move. Soon we will all finally be in control of Heaven and there will be no more scraping by in this pit. Love, Amauros.'"

"He did not write 'Love, Amauros' did he?" Ted, one of the demons asked.

"Of course he did!" snapped Chrissy. "Do you think I'm pathetic enough to just say that? Like I need some kind of validation that I'm loved?!"

"I'm just saying that that's not like him. He has a hard time expressing emotion. And he's the Duke of Hell. Also, on a side note: how the hell are you going to replace BJ? You are a giant monster. He is a well dressed black man." Ted retorted.

Fucking Ted. Chrissy hated Ted.

"Don't forget he's still my twin brother. Amauros told me that the closer I get to Heaven, the closer I will get to my original form. I just have to get to that waiting room. That should be close enough."

The demon's ears perked up. None of them had seen their true selves since they had died, and for a couple of them that had been a long time. The thought of seeing themselves again made them giddy with excitement. Well, all except for Ted. Ted was fucking ugly.

NINE

The normally bustling orientation room was eerily dark and empty. The usual chatter of keyboards was replaced with an unsettling silence. Colin was taken aback as he walked in. He expected everyone to be there, and more than that, he expected some sort of explanation regarding the attack that happened fifteen minutes ago.

"Where is everyone?" Brad asked

"I don't know. Maybe they are all in their rooms?" Colin responded. "It sounds like the angels got everything cleaned up out there. I wonder why the lights are still off."

The room was illuminated only by the blank glares of computer screens and the light over the waiting room door at the other end of the room. It must have been powered by some back up generator or something. Colin walked over to the window and pensively opened the blinds.

"I don't see anything going on outside. Something doesn't seem right about all of this," Colin said.

"What do you mean?" Brad asked.

"I've heard of demons attacking before. That doesn't seem that farfetched. I'm sure that they would love to get into one of these buildings and shut it down. Without us taking care of our clients they could be doing all kinds of damage on earth. It'd be like shooting fish in a barrel."

"So what doesn't seem right then? They attacked. The angels kicked them out. No problems."

"That's what I mean. There was barely any effort at all. The demons just ran straight up the street. They didn't seem to have any plan or any kind of goal. They just ran through the open and let the angels kick them out with barely a fight."

"Well, the angels are kind of bad ass. I don't really think that any of those demons could pose any kind of real threat to them."

"Yeah, that's true, but what are the odds of all the different divisions out there, all the different buildings, and all of the demons that Purgatory could send, they would send the same creature that killed me to the same building that I'm in, this close to the time that my Watcher would be getting into Heaven? Something is not adding up here."

Colin was startled by the sound of the door opening. In walked a man dressed in white with an uncharacteristically stern look on his face. Colin recognized him as Director Hauser. Next to him was Leah. Colin was always nervous around her. She was beautiful and had an easy air to her. Her red hair was tied back, and she had a purpose in her eyes.

Colin would see Director Hauser around the building once in a while. He was a good man who always seemed to have a smile on his face. Even in the aftermath of an attack by a legion of demons, he seemed pretty chipper.

"Hey there, fellas. What are you two doing here?" He asked.

"We heard the alarms and we weren't sure where to

go. What is going on outside?" Colin questioned back. "Is the attack over?"

"Yes, everything is safe now. You two can go back to your rooms. We have a crew heading to the basement and they will be getting the power back on very soon."

"There was a monster that led the attack. I recognized him. During the battle he disappeared. What happened to him? Did the angels get him out?" Colin asked nervously.

"To which creature are you referring?" Director Hauser said.

"Uh...well he was pretty big and scary looking. He had pointy ears," Colin answered.

"It was an army of demons from Hell. You're gonna have to be a bit more specific."

Colin explained his story. He told Director Hauser of his death and about the attempt by someone from Limbo to stop it. He mentioned that his name was BJ.

"Leah…" Director Hauser turned toward her. "Pull up Colin's info, and find this BJ guy. We need to get him out of the waiting room and figure out what he knows."

Leah sent one of the computers to life and slid gracefully into the desk chair in front. There was an uncomfortable wait as the keyboard took the beating from her fingers as she searched for information on BJ.

"I'm not finding anything about anyone with that name..,"" she said as she looked up from the screen. "Let me check another system…"

Colin was confused. He knew what he heard, granted it was nearly three decades ago, but you don't forget the day you're stabbed by a monster.

"Wait..," she said. "I found him. He's in section 2C."

"Leah, could you please go get him?" Director Hauser politely ordered.

She stood up and headed toward the waiting room.

* * * * *

The waiting room was buzzing with nervous chatter. BJ shifted in his chair as the alarms rang through the air. The waiting room was the size of hundreds of gymnasiums. It was filled with a countless number of chairs, tables and TV's. There were coffee stands and food kiosks. Tents and canopies were set up all around. People were offering various wares and goods, all handmade. It was like a humongous flea market inside of an airport terminal. If you were to look down on the waiting room, you would notice that it was laid out in a shape that almost resembles a sea shell. Toward what would be the base of the sea shell, the room funneled into an enormous, golden doorway. Above the door an enormous marquee sign changed names.

The names flashed for a moment and he swore he saw his name appear.

BJ tried to shake the confusion away. *That can't be. I still have a couple days left.* He looked around, unsure what to do. Everyone was so preoccupied with the alarms that no one noticed the name change. A red headed woman appeared to his side.

"Time to go," she said. "We need to get you out of here."

BJ wasn't sure how to respond, but it didn't matter because before he had a chance to, Leah had him on his feet and was escorting him toward the door back to the orientation room.

At that moment the lights went out and the alarm was silenced. Murmurs of confusion were the only thing audible.

"What the heck is going on here, lady? I've been

sitting in that waiting room for almost thirty years and I've never seen them lights go out. In fact, I've been asking what kind of light bulbs you all use," BJ said in a desperate hush.

"We will fill you in when we get out of the waiting room," Leah said as they rushed toward the exit through the dark. The other souls that were waiting for their turn began lighting candles and flashlights, making the enormous space seem more like a cave than a waiting room.

"Wait, the door is the other way. We're heading backwards. Who are you? What is going on here?" BJ asked.

"My name is Leah. I am in charge of Troubleshooting. We have to get you out of here so we can seal this room up. Then, we have to get to the orientation room and figure out where to hide you," she responded.

Hide me? Shit, is my ex-wife here? Can't be that, surely she went to Hell.

TEN

Everyone jumped as the waiting room door slid open. BJ and Leah walked into the orientation room. BJ glanced around the room with a sense of nostalgia. This room had changed so much since he had left for the waiting room. He looked at Director Hauser and scanned the rest of the guys. He froze when he saw Colin.

BJ looked over at Leah, knowingly.

"Oh no. It's my brother, isn't it?" he asked.

"That's what we are hoping you can help with. Let's just take a seat." She turned toward Colin and Brad. "You two should probably go back to your rooms. Thank you for your help, but it'd probably be best…"

Just then the lights came back on and the rest of the computers began to whir to life. Everyone seemed to be relieved. Two more men dressed in white joined them from the halls.

BJ interrupted. "You don't know me, I'm sure," he said to Colin.

Colin shook his head, but he had a gut feeling that it was him.

"We never got a chance to meet in person. I was your Watcher. Before you died, in a pretty badass way I might add, I was your guy. I probably know you better than anyone."

Colin couldn't help but feel a touch of guilt. He had been a Watcher himself now for 28 years and he understood the bond you develop for your client. He always knew that it was a one sided affection, but he never really considered that if he were to meet Jack right now, he would be a complete stranger. It was heartbreaking.

"I, uh..." Colin started.

"It's alright, cat," BJ shrugged off. "I didn't expect to see you for a long time."

Director Hauser interrupted, "We need to get all of you into a safe place until we can verify the location of BJ's brother. At this point it's safe to assume that he is the target on this attack."

At that the lights went out again. It didn't feel right to Colin. He was beginning to regret leaving his room. *This isn't good.*

"The basement..." Director Hauser said to the two men that walked in with him. "You two go check it out please."

The two men turned their flashlights on and began walking toward the exit. As one of them reached for the handle, the doors burst open and the force sent the men flailing back like ragdolls. Everyone froze in terror as they watched the demons begin to pour into the door. Chrissy followed and began to snarl as he saw his brother. Leah jumped to action and ran toward the fire alarm on the wall. One of the demons jumped at her and with one backhanded slap sent her to the ground hard.

"Run!" Director Hauser yelled as he began sprinting for the waiting room. The demons were tailing him.

Chrissy watched as the people began to scramble. He knew they had made a mistake. This was not part of the plan. There was no way of just replacing his brother with none the wiser. It was time to call an audible.

"Stop him!" Chrissy screamed.

Hauser was almost to the doors. There was a protocol for this kind of thing. He knew that the waiting room had a lockdown procedure, and he was one of the few people in the building who had the code.

The demons couldn't catch up to him in time. He slammed his hands on to the keypad and entered the code, thus locking down the waiting room. Without hesitation, Chrissy picked up a computer screen and threw it across the room, striking the director in the back of the head. BJ grabbed a frozen Colin, and they began to run. Brad was already at the side door motioning for them to hurry.

"We have to get out of here!" BJ said.

They darted into the hall and began to run for the stairs. One of the benefits of being a dead person was not having the need to breathe. You don't get tired either. This really comes in handy when being chased by scary-ass demons from Hell. However, being dead also increases the odds of being chased by scary-ass demons from Hell. It's an even trade.

As the group of Watchers made their way to the first floor of the Rocky Mountain Division, they could hear the creatures echoing from the top of the stairs.

"What do we do?!" Colin said in a frenzy.

"Follow me. We can hide in the caves!" BJ responded.

Colin had never been in the caves, but he had heard stories about them. Everyone in Limbo knew about the caves. There are pathways in them that connect Limbo and Purgatory, but supposedly there are other pathways, too. Some that lead to all kinds of different places, even back to earth. However, they were strictly forbidden to all residents.

As they ran out the front door they heard a deafening crash above them. Shards of glass were raining down on them as one of the creatures came jumping out of the window. They turned the corner of the building and started off toward the rear and into the fields behind.

"The caves are just at the end of this field!" BJ yelled.

Colin took a moment to look back behind him. There were two demons still on the chase. They were a football field away but they weren't slowing down.

"What do they want with you, BJ?! They can't kill us! We're already dead!" Colin asked

"There are worse things than death in these realms, cat," BJ said as they ran.

As they approached the caves, they could feel the cold air coming from the openings.

"I haven't been in these things for a long time, but I doubt much has changed," BJ said as they walked through the mouth of the closest cave to them. The light from the entrance disappeared with every step.

"Be careful where you step." he said. "There are holes in these caves that will take you to places you DO NOT want to go."

They slowed their pace and began down a narrow path over a deep abyss. The sounds of running water echoed in the distance.

The three of them moved quietly.

"I think we lost them," Brad whispered.

"Let's find a place to wait for a little bit," BJ responded.

They continued down the treacherous rocky bridge hoping for some sort refuge inside the spooky cavern.

"I know you are in here," echoed a voice that could only belong to one of the monsters pursuing them. It was deep and gravelly. "Come on out, and let's get back to the building. I won't hurt you. I promise."

The group froze. They could feel the creature getting closer and closer with each empty promise it made. They could hear the sounds of flowing water getting louder in the dark abyss below. If there wasn't a Hellish monster looking for them, it would have been kind of tranquil. The path took them to the edge of a giant pit. They leaned on the wall to help stay balanced.

The creature turned the corner and caught eyes with his targets. He let out a deafening scream and began running toward them. In a panic, the group started stumbling over each other as they turned to run. BJ slipped on a rock and hit the ground hard. The impact broke the rocks away and he started to fall as the floor crumbled away. Instantly, Colin grabbed his arm and stopped him from plummeting into the unknown below.

BJ reached his other hand up and began to try and climb back to his feet. The creature was on them before he could make any progress. Brad was hit first. The demon ran through him like a linebacker on the snap. He bounced off the cavern wall and lost consciousness. The fear and adrenaline were too much for Colin, and he lost his balance, letting go of BJ at the same time. BJ grasped the air as he was trying to hold on to anything he could. Before the demon could grab them, they were both falling through the dark.

The monster stared down the abyss looking for signs of his prey. With no hope of finding them, he angrily grabbed Brad by the leg and began dragging him back to the division.

Colin and BJ were falling through the unknown. It was a long drop. Until they hit the water, Colin was beginning to think that they were not going to land. The water was warm. It was like landing in a bath with a slow, steady current.

"What do we do now?!" Colin asked as he spit water out of his mouth.

"We don't really have much of a choice but to float, motherfucker!" BJ responded.

As they floated down the cavernous stream, they calmed down a little. There were a lot of questions going through Colin's head and he was hoping BJ had the answers. The water started moving faster as they were getting closer to what appeared to be a very small hole. It was just big enough for one person to fit through.

"Looks like this is our exit!" BJ said as he braced for impact.

They watched the opening get closer and closer, faster and faster. As they came upon it, they could make out one of the demons on the cave walls high above. He had a large stone in his hand and was hammering at the rocks causing them to break away from the wall.

"He's trying to cave us in!" BJ shouted. "Cover your head!"

Rocks began to fall from above as they neared the exit. Each impact made a large splash. It was going to be close. Colin braced for the crash. The two went under as they were sucked through the opening, rocks falling all around them. Once through, they could see something that they haven't seen in a long time. Sunlight poked into them like pins and needles. Then they started to fall again.

ELEVEN

When Jack was eighteen years old, he had received a scholarship for swimming, so naturally, he went to college. It was a year of complete debauchery and soul searching as he went through the motions of a freshman in a stale academia. He took basic general education classes. He thought maybe he'd major in engineering. He was good at math. Why not? His father was very proud.

He moved into a six bed suite in the oldest dorm building on campus where he made some new friends and was joined by two friends from high school, Tony and Tyson. Then there were the new guys. There was Chris Mudd, whom he had never met awake, Mark Neumann, who was a dirty trucker incarnate, and Aaron Bruns, a fragile little dude who was caught numerous times visiting Grannygetsnaked.com.

It was a dusty band of vagrants, with Jack as their mantle piece. He was born with the gift of having a good time, but college gave him all the tools he needed to perfect the party. As Jack discovered more of his gift with the party, he lost more and more interest in school. *I can learn more in the world than I can from a math book* he would think.

He wrote music. He read. He meditated.

There were parties. There were girls. There were bad decisions. However, Jack used his musical abilities for good rather than douchery. There were a lot of guys with nice hair that could play a guitar and sing along with the best bedroom voice they could muster, but Jack was a poet. He wrote of angst and fire. He sang about balls and dirt. He longed for the hardship if for only a chance to see the real world with clear eyes.

Over the course of two semesters, his grades began to slip. He focused more on his music and less and less on the books. He stopped going to some of his classes altogether. College was a waste of his time.

After swim practice, Jack would walk across campus and feel pity for the students around him. *All this money to get a degree for a job that they probably don't even want* he would think. *Life is about experiences. I ain't gonna die with a full tank of gas.*

He walked into the floor of his dorm. The room attendant was sitting at the front desk. He was wearing a Superman t-shirt. He had spikey blonde hair and stood painfully erect, as if to say to the world: I am douche. Hear me roar.

"Hello, Jack," he would say with a thin veneer of kindness.

"Yo," Jack would answer with honest disinterest. They both regarded each other as fuck-ups.

The elevator gave a ding and Jack strolled inside. He pushed the fourth floor button and leaned against the wall. Elevators always made him feel cool.

The dorm suite was quiet, except for the gentle tapping of a keyboard from Aaron's desk. He was in his bedroom, either looking at porn or doing homework, sometimes both. Aaron was a skinny little rich kid from

Minneapolis. There was a nasally tone to his voice that would drive the others crazy. Every "I'm cold" or "turn the music down" or "don't bring girls in here" drove Jack insane.

Jack walked into the kitchen and grabbed some rice cakes from the cupboard. He sat on the couch and began to munch. It was 11 am, and he hadn't eaten anything yet.

Tyson and Tony walked in together.

"Jacky, what's poppin'?" Tony would say with a goofball smile. They set their bags down against the wall. Tyson reached up into the ceiling panel and pulled out a couple beers.

They joined Jack on the couch. The Xbox whirred to life as they picked up the controllers.

"Jack, can you stop crunching so loudly? I'm trying to study!" Aaron whined from the back room.

"It's a rice cake, Aaron. There's gonna be a crunch. Not much I can do about it," Jack responded with his eyes rolled.

"It's distracting me. Can you soften it with water or something?"

"No, Aaron, then it would be a soggy rice cake. That sounds terrible, man."

"I'm surprised you even know what 'soften' means!" Tony joined in "What with all that granny porn you watch in there."

"I don't watch granny porn!" Aaron fired back.

"Sure man. Whatever you say." Tony focused back on the Xbox.

"Just put some headphones on!" Tyson yelled while keeping his eyes on the TV screen.

"I can't think with music. Just be quiet in there," Aaron whined again.

Jack took another bite. He crunched down slowly,

hoping to dampen the sound a bit.

"I can still hear you!" Aaron whined again melodically.

Jack couldn't take it anymore. He grabbed a few more rice cakes and walked to Aaron's doorway. He stood in silence and stared at the back of Aaron's head, contemplating shoving one of the cakes into his ears.

CRUNCH! Jack bit down as hard as he could, letting crumbs drop to the floor.

Aaron turned around. "HEY!" he yelled "You have to clean that up!"

"No I don't," Jack said, still chewing.

Aaron was stunned. "Yes, you do. You're making a mess in MY room."

CRUNCH!

"Jack! Stop!"

"What do you have against rice cakes, Aaron?" Jack asked the whiny little dude.

"You're being obnoxious."

"So?"

"I'll go get the RA."

"Why don't you just have a rice cake, Aaron? Here." Jack reached a cake out toward him.

"No. I don't want one," Aaron whined. "Please get out of my room. I'm busy."

"Don't you like rice cakes, Aaron?"

"Leave me alone."

"I want you to eat a rice cake."

"No! I don't like them."

"How can you not like them? They're delicious."

"I just don't like them! Go AWAY!"

"Have you ever tried a rice cake before, Aaron?" Jack was determined.

"No." Aaron turned back to his desk.

"Well how do you know you don't like them if you've

never tried one? Doesn't make much sense, does it?"

"I just don't."

"Eat a fucking rice cake, Aaron."

"JACK, GO AWAY!"

"Just take one bite and I'll leave you alone."

"NO!"

Jack moved near him and spun his chair around. He grabbed him out of the chair and forced him to the ground. He held one arm on his chest, pinning him down; the other had a rice cake pointed toward his mouth. Aaron squirmed, with his mouth shut as tight as he could keep it.

"JUST ONE RICE CAKE, AARON! EAT IT!" Jack began to yell.

"NO!"

"EAT IT!"

"NO!!"

"EAT THE RICE CAKE!"

"I DON'T WANT TO!"

"EAT THE FUCKING CAKE GOD DAMN IT!"

"JACK, GET OFF OF ME!"

Jack ignored the voice in his head, telling him to leave the poor kid alone. Aaron's freckles were accented by the increasing red in his face. The others heard the commotion and came to the doorway to watch this unfold.

"DO IT!"

"NO!"

"I swear to Christ, Aaron, this rice cake is going inside you one way or the other. You decide which hole!"

There was a moment of silence. Then a light *crunch* was the only thing audible. Aaron whimpered as he chewed the rice cake down and swallowed. Jack stood up.

"They're good right? You're welcome," He said as he

walked into his bedroom and started packing his things.

Tony and Tyson followed him. They weren't sure what to think.

"What are you doing?" Tony asked.

"Packing," Jack said as he closed his guitar case and put on his shoes.

"Where you going?" Tony said with some slight confusion.

"I think I'm done wasting my time with college."

He walked to the door, guitar in hand and a few backpacks on his shoulders. He snagged a beer from the ceiling and cracked it open.

"Later, dudes," Jack said and walked out the door. His semester was over. The two stood there in awe.

When the coast was clear, Aaron snuck into the kitchen and grabbed another rice cake out of the cupboard. They were delicious.

Twelve

Purina.

He could feel the wet heat of a panting dog on his face as it licked his cheeks. Colin was on his back. He opened his eyes.

Purina.

He could hear the rapid breathing as the dog over exaggerated a smile inches from his ears. This is not how a man should be brought back to consciousness: by a joyful, slobbering labradoodle.

Purina.

He could smell the dog food on the beast's breath. It was absolutely disgusting. He flew into life and pushed the crossbreed's face away from his.

"Gah! Nasty!" he shouted.

The pup stepped back, looked at him, then in a flash, leapt forward and gave him one last kiss before running off into some nearby woods. Thoughts and anxiety were rushing through Colin's head. *Where am I?* Something felt different and vaguely familiar at the same time.

"BJ!" he shouted to no response.

He didn't remember much after the fall. Basically he just fell for a long time, which isn't all that exciting if you think about it. His clothes were dry, which led him to believe that he had been unconscious for quite a while. He also had no shoes, and in the midst of all the excitement he couldn't remember if he had lost them, or if he had forgotten to put any on to begin with.

Shoes weren't really a popular item in Limbo. This was for two reasons: utility and convention. First of all, why the heck would you need shoes in Limbo? You wake up when your client wakes up. You make some coffee (another unnecessary, but if you don't want coffee in the afterlife, then you may as well go murder a nun while listening to Van Halen, because you belong in Hell.) You put on some comfy clothes, and you begin your journey through righteousness. It's a simple life with simple pleasures, and the latest pair of Reeboks isn't really on the wish list. That is, unless of course you find yourself running through a dimly lit, rocky cavern, evading demons from Hell.

Secondly, Jesus did not wear shoes. He wore sandals in life obviously, but he is almost always barefoot, and Jesus is a fucking trend-setter.

Where am I? Colin looked around. He was laying on the shore of a very small pond. There was a rocky entrance just above the water to his side. It was blocked by what appeared to be a cave in.

The shadows of the trees were getting closer and closer to their base. It was almost noon. The labradoodle drool that remained on his cheek felt cool against the soft breeze. Colin wiped his face and stood up. He had to find BJ. He had to find Jack. He had to find a way back to Limbo.

"BJ! Where the hell are you?!"

He heard some rustling to his left. He turned and started toward some shrubbery. The bushes were moving in a smooth and explorative manner, almost like a black jazz musician was stuck inside of them.

"Help me out of here, cat," the bush said.

Colin began sifting through the branches looking for a way out. It seemed as if BJ had landed on the hill behind and rolled into the backside of the bushes. Colin walked around and pulled his companion to freedom.

"Thanks for that," BJ said.

In the light of things, Colin couldn't help but be amused.

"Where are we?" Colin asked

"You got me," BJ responded. "Let's take a walk and try to figure it out."

They began walking downhill, hoping to find any kind of landmark that may give them a clue as to where they were. The woods weren't too deep, and they found themselves in a clearing before long.

"The day that I was killed you were there, weren't you? I heard your voice when I was in the mineshaft," Colin asked as they stepped into the field.

"Yeah. I saw what was happening and I snuck out of the division to try and talk some sense into Chrissy."

"So he's your brother?"

BJ nodded, "Yes. He's my twin brother and has always been a pain in my ass. Even in death it seems."

"How did you get to Earth? Through those caves?"

"Yeah. There are a few different ways to get between worlds. But seeing as how our entrance has been caved in…looks like we need to find another way back."

"So where do we need to go to get back home?"

"I'm not sure. We need to find a way to communicate with the cats back home. I don't even know where we are, but I can definitely say that this sunshine feels familiar."

"How do you know all of this? I have been in Limbo for twenty-eight years, and I have never heard about the caves or coming back to earth or anything like this!"

"You have never visited the library? There are literally thousands of documents that explain all of this."

"Of course I've been to the library."

He hadn't.

They walked in silence for a little while. Neither of them was used to the whole using your lungs thing. As they walked over a hill they came on top of a clearing. The Rocky Mountains stood before them like a gigantic painting in the horizon. It stopped them both in their tracks.

"I remember the mountains being beautiful," Colin said "But after twenty-eight years I didn't realize how much I missed them until now. It's funny how you can take something so incredibly beautiful for granted."

"You're right. I always wondered how a person could have something so perfect and majestic at their disposal, and totally forget to appreciate it every day. The Rocky Mountains, or the ocean, or an incredible piece of architecture or a perfect butt in a short skirt just bouncing the night way." BJ agreed.

They looked across the field from their overlook and saw highway 70. As huge as the mountains looked, they were still miles and miles away.

"I guess it's safe to say that we are in Colorado," Colin mentioned.

BJ nodded. They both took a breath and headed toward the road.

"We need to find a ride," BJ said.

"We need to find Jack," Colin replied. "We could have

been out for a while. Who knows what he's gotten himself into?"

They slowly walked on the shoulder of the highway, with thumbs out. Eventually a man in an old Subaru Outback saw them and pulled over to the side of the road.

"Heading to Denver?" the old man asked.

"Yes sir, Lakewood in particular," Colin replied.

"Right on. Hop in."

*   *   *   *   *

Olivia regretted answering the phone.

"Well how many songs has he written, Olivia?"

"How many homes have you built, Jack?"

"You can't build a home; you can only build a house, Olivia."

Jack spiked the phone down triumphantly. Olivia was being an incredibly huge beyotch toward him since the breakup. They were together for four years, which doesn't seem like a very long time, but those four short years were made of iron. He wasn't sure why he called her. He reasoned that he couldn't find one of his notebooks and wondered if she still had it. The real reason was that something was pushing him to call her and pick a fight. He couldn't help himself.

Jack and Olivia met when he was 23 years old. He was opening the bar at Pepper's Bar and Grill when she walked in. As he watched her approach the bar everything around her became blurry. There was nothing else to focus on but her. The freckles, the light behind her eyes, the legs, that was all he could see.

"Hi, I'm here for my interview," she crooned. Her voice was poetry. Her words were music. Jack was dazed.

"Interview for what?" he asked.

"Well, a job I hope," she quipped.

"Oh! Yeah, I knew that. Yep, the boss and I are pretty tight. He was just telling me about the new candidates." That was a lie. The boss hated Jack thanks to a fourteen hour tequila bender from a few months back, but that's a story in itself.

"Yeah, he said that when you got here to tell you to sit at that table in the corner. So… go sit at that table in the corner."

"OK, thanks! I'm Olivia by the way."

"Jack." He reached out his hand.

"Nice to meet you, Jack." Olivia took his hand.

The second he heard her say his name he was in love. The second he touched her hand he was completely screwed.

Olivia's new boyfriend was a polar opposite of Jack. He owned his own construction business, was well to do financially, had stability at home, and a fantastic beard. None of those things were ever important to Jack, though. What mattered to him was the story. He wanted to leave a mark on the world. He was a songwriter and an amateur philosopher. A self appointed poet laureate in an over processed world. Jack felt that in this life you can build things up and burn things down, but a song lasts forever. You can't break a song.

Damn my ex is a bitch. Jack stumbled down the stairs to the basement of the band house in Lakewood. There was a piano in the corner of the room that was calling his name. *Is there a reason she needs to constantly remind me of her new boyfriend?* He sat on the stool and lifted the wooden cover that protected the keys. His fingers slowly walked their way down toward the low C. *She's such a fucking beyotch.* As they reached their target they came across a plastic baggie that was placed upon the ivories. Jack snatched the baggie up and from it he pulled some mushrooms.

"I wish I could play this thing," he said as he slammed the piano cover shut. "One day I'll learn, but until then..," he held the baggie in front of his face, "you and I are about to take a journey, my little shroomtroopers." And with that, Jack ate a large amount of psychedelic mushrooms.

Two hours later, the ground shook beneath Jack's feet. There was what sounded like an explosion outside, and every dog within miles was howling at the moon. Jack began to walk upstairs to investigate the situation, but immediately forgot what he was doing midway up. *I wonder who figured stairs out. A fucking genius, that's who!* He stood on the stairs for a while and continued his trip.

THIRTEEN

Two hours earlier...

Spanish Cave in Custer County, Colorado, has an insane depth of 741 feet. The heart of the cave is known as The Jug and The Pit. Here one can find relics of expeditions throughout the last century. There are hammers, and ropes, and ladders. There's even a skeleton or two, remains of past treasure seekers putting it all on the line for their chance at the legendary Spanish gold hidden there: The treasure of La Caverna del Oro.

This was not why Blaine and Zelda Falconer were here. In fact, if they had known the ridiculous depth of this particular cave they would have come back to earth through any other one. The climb was difficult for most experience cavers, let alone two ancient demons that had spent most of their time living in the plains of Nebraska.

The changes that take place during your time in Hell and Purgatory may dull one's mind, rendering them into dumb, sometimes hairy, sometimes scaly monsters, but the physical effects more often than not give incredible strength. This helped the two with their climb out.

Demons are always pretty sweaty, but these two were almost dripping when they reached the surface.

Zelda crawled into the sunlight first. She rolled over and lay on her back, catching her newly returned breath. Blaine fell down beside her. A faded red cross marked the cavern entrance next to them.

"GOD DAMN! We picked the wrong entrance," Blaine said, breathing heavily.

"How are we going to get to Lakewood? We have to find the Watchers before they find the songwriter." Zelda asked.

"I know it. Can we take a second to catch our breath?!" Blaine rolled over.

"How are we going to find them?" Zelda continued.

"GOD, ALL YOU EVER DO IS NAG!" Blaine was annoyed.

The two had lived most of their lives together just west of Omaha. They were high school sweethearts and eventually got married at the ripe age of twenty one years old. They never had kids and didn't regret it. They never had pets, but Zelda always wanted a cat. Their life of crime began shortly after the wedding, while on a trip to the grocery store. While waiting to pay, the clerk had to find the supervisor to apply a discount. He left the register open when he walked away, and Blaine couldn't help himself. He reached over the counter and grabbed as many bills as he could fit in both hands. The couple ran away as fast as they could.

It was such a rush that they decided to do it again. Before they knew it, they were holding up liquor stores and breaking into cars.

Life was good for a while, but eventually the prospect of living a life of crime together was beginning to wear on them. They began to bicker and argue. The love was fading.

The crime spree came to a halt when they decided to go for a big score. They were going to rob an armored truck as it made its regular stop at the local bank. The plan was simple and solid. They would jump out and stop the truck three blocks away from the bank. Zelda would hold the guards up while Blaine would grab as much money as he could. The two would split ways, and meet at their usual spot outside of town: simple and solid.

However, Zelda's mother was visiting for the weekend, and the two were on edge and not quite in sync with each other. They were still bickering at each other when they jumped in front of the vehicle, shotguns pointed at the driver side.

Coincidentally, the driver of the armored truck's mother-in-law was also in town visiting, and he, too, was a little distracted. He didn't even notice the married couple jumping out in front of his truck and ran them right over, killing them instantly.

When they were sentenced to Hell, their punishment was to continue being married to each other.

Amauros had been watching things unfold and recruited the two demons to find Colin and BJ before they could cause any more problems with his plans. He was already unsure of how long they could keep the Rocky Mountain Division under lock before they were found out. He was nervous, which was unusual, which made him angry.

*　　*　　*　　*　　*

Blaine stood up, dusted himself off, and looked around. There was a path ahead of them; most likely it led to a parking lot.

"This way."

Zelda was already standing. They started down the path. A dirty gold coin bounced away as Zelda unknowingly kicked it.

There were only a few cars in the lot, with no one to be seen. They started looking through the vehicles for any spare key. Zelda popped the metal gas tank cover open on an old teal Ford Windstar. A hide-a-key was held on the inside by a magnetic strip. She slid the top open and found a key to the van.

The van came to life. Blaine walked over to the driver seat.

"I'll drive," he said.

"I'm already in the driver seat, hop in," Zelda responded back as she was adjusting the mirrors.

"You're a terrible driver," he told her.

"What? Who totaled the pickup?" She fired back.

"That's not fair! I was drunk!" Blaine argued.

"Well, what else was new?! You were ALWAYS drunk!"

"You know you're acting just like your mother."

"You're a real asshole, you know that?"

Rocks shuffled in the parking lot as a man froze in his tracks staring at the two bickering demons. He had just finished a hike around the area and was holding his car keys. The demons both paused the argument and stared back at the guy.

"Which one of these is yours?" Blaine asked the guy. His voice had a hiss and a pop, like an old scratchy record.

"The Honda..," the hiker responded. He was scared shitless.

"Perfect," Blaine answered.

Minutes later, the Windstar was cruising down the

highway with the windows down. Zelda was wearing some sunglasses she found in the center console and had the radio up loud.

Behind her was Blaine in his newly commandeered Honda Passport. He'd be damned again if he wasn't gonna drive. They took the next exit and merged onto Highway 76 toward Lakewood, Colorado.

* * * * *

Brad woke up in the boiler room. He was chained to a brick wall. The smooth concrete floor was cold against his bare feet. As he looked around, he could see the demons sitting at a table, playing cards. Director Hauser, Leah, and the other workers from the observation room were chained to the wall as well.

The elevator opened and Chrissy walked in. The demons turned to him and they began to talk in hushed voices. After their Hellish huddle, they broke. Chrissy and half a dozen demons went back to the elevator, while two other demons headed toward the exit.

"They have everyone locked in their quarters," Director Hauser whispered to everyone. "Limbo has become a prison."

"BJ and Colin... we tried to escape to the caves. They..," Brad began to explain, "they fell."

"They could be anywhere," Leah said. "But right now we need to figure out how to get control back over Limbo. Things could get messy back on Earth very soon."

* * * * *

It was dark when the Subaru squeaked as it pulled in

front of Jack's house in Lakewood. It was a run down neighborhood on the south side of Denver. Many of the houses were either completely empty, or overrun with family members.

"Thank you so much for the ride," Colin said. "And good luck with your bong shop!"

BJ also thanked the driver as they got out of the car and looked toward Jack's house. It was large. It used to be a duplex until the members of The Devil Wears Nada decided it was in their best interest to all share a house. They converted the second kitchen into a grow room and all moved in.

As the two Watchers of Limbo walked toward the front door, they noticed piles of garbage bags on the side of the house. The sun had gone down a few hours ago, and a red full moon was shining through the sky like a glowing ember. The light bouncing off of the black plastic bags gave Colin the strangest feeling that maybe there was more than meets the eye. He could have sworn they were moving, but couldn't decide if it was the moon playing tricks on him or if being back on Earth was making him tired.

The house seemed much larger on the outside than one would think. The worn down wooden siding was faded by the sun. The aftermath of a post-show party left the metal handrail that had once guided a boozed up rocker safely up the concrete stairs and to the front door bent at a ninety degree angle. Silver beer cans scattered in the yard reflected the light from the streetlamps in the street. It reminded Colin of a trashy frat house. He knew that Jack was the furthest from a frat boy that he could think of, but he felt that the two types just might share a common bond in the quest for a good time.

They could smell the fumes of gasoline as they passed

by a couple red canisters on the driveway. There was an old beat up black truck parked there with the windows rolled down. Colin felt that it was silly to leave your windows rolled down in a neighborhood like this, but in reality, the "dangerous types" that shared this 'hood were much more frightened of the rock and roll household than vice versa.

They approached the concrete steps and heard the rustle behind them. It came from the side of the house.

The garbage bags! Colin immediately knew that he was right. Just then the night exploded into a frenzy of demonic screams. The bags were tossed away with a Hellish strength and two demons jumped out and began to run toward them.

The first one hit BJ before he could turn around. The force sent him over the bent hand rails, adding another couple degrees to the angle. Colin grabbed a beer bottle from the yard and swung it in time to connect with the second demon before it got on top of him. The force broke the bottle and sent pain through Colin's hand. The demon staggered backwards and tripped over the gas canisters, spilling gasoline into the driveway. The pool quickly flowed toward the fallen demon and made contact with his foot, which immediately went up in flames. The blaze sent the demon scrambling away toward the street but not until he was completely engulfed and instantly dissipated in a flash of light. A Hellish scream that echoed through the streets was all that remained.

They're flammable! He ran back to the gas canisters, picked one up and ran to BJ. He was still wrestling with the other demon in the yard.

"Zelda! No!" the demon cried out as he punched BJ in the stomach. The impact sent him tumbling away.

Colin popped the lid and splashed gas on the

creatures back. He immediately went up in flames. He let out a horrible screech and began to run into the nearby driveway, crashing right into the side of black truck. The creature disappeared with a flash in the same way, but left the truck on fire. It exploded almost instantly. The sound was deafening and sent Colin and BJ back a few feet. Dogs began barking and howling within a square mile. Colin could see the lights come on in the neighboring houses. They scrambled to the side of the house and into the back yard.

"Who needs holy water?" Colin said as he caught his breath.

The back door flew open and Jack stepped out into the moonlight. A cigarette glowed in his left hand. His brows were furrowed and a hawk like gaze swept the darkness. Sweatpants were rolled up to his knees, and the light reflected off of his bare chest. The mushrooms hadn't yet worn off, and although Jack was used to the trips, an exploding truck in his driveway wasn't helping him come down. He noticed the smoldering remains.

He ran to the garden hose and turned it on.

"Shit shit shit shit shit shit shit shit shit."

The hose was long enough to go around the side of the house and he began to fight the fire with the vengeance of a gardener. The water was pouring out of the hose with a very underwhelming force. The trip grabbed hold of him again for a moment and he stopped watering down the flaming vehicle. He looked around to make sure that Dave's truck was, in fact, on fire. He reached out toward it and the flames nipped his hand. *YEP, IT'S BURNING!*

"Dave is going to KILL ME. Oh man, he loves this truck. Oh man, this isn't good."

FOURTEEN

Catfish Durham was asleep in his regular alley of Blake and 16th Street when he felt his bag moving. He lay perfectly still and pretend to still be asleep. He found an old bike chain months ago that he began using to secure his bag of things to himself as he slept at night. Thanks to this chain link security system he wasn't too worried about losing his things, but he was determined to give this would-be thief the scare of his street urchin life. This was his alley and most of the regular street guys knew this. Whoever was trying to rob him was either new to the area, drunk, crazy, or a combination of the three.

Maybe it's Mick E Mouse messing with me? The bag began to jerk him as it was being tugged at harder and harder. Still he feigned sleep. *This son of a bitch better be ready.*

He had been on the streets for a while now. It had been at least seven years since his first night outside. It was a brutal world that is all too often swept under the rug of society, but after so long, Catfish knew no other way of life than to be a crumb. The other street guys were OK. Some of them were not to be trusted, but there was a sort of brotherhood between them. It was a different life with different names and different goals.

Durham grew up in the northern suburbs of Minneapolis. His mother died when he was very young and his father was a good man. He worked two jobs and gave his son nice clothes, a car on his sixteenth birthday, and helped as much as he could with college tuition. Durham always felt a little disconnected with the world, but he always shrugged it off as a normal thing. School was a challenge, but after years of studying marketing he finished his degree at University of Minnesota. At 23, he started a good job with a marketing firm that specialized in insurance plans. He moved in with his girlfriend. Life had a good path set ahead of him.

One day he was drinking some coffee at his desk when he noticed his hands. His hands seemed different. He couldn't stop looking at them. It was hard to place exactly what was changing, but something was different, and it didn't feel right.

Things started changing at work, and a lot of new faces began to appear. Durham was sure that it had something to do with him. He noticed the food began to taste differently in the cafeteria, and his work emails started having mysterious text in them. Something wasn't right, and his damned hands, they were changing more and more all the time.

He stopped eating the food and began to keep track of his co-workers' whereabouts throughout the office. He no longer went to lunch with colleagues or gave his input at meetings. They weren't interested in his work. They wanted to test him. They wanted to experiment on his hands. There was something wrong with them.

He lost a lot of weight. His girlfriend, Kate, began to worry about him. She started asking questions and mentioned that his boss had called her, with a similar worry. *She is in on it, too! The bastards are using her against me!*

His heart was broken. He stopped going in to work and realized the only one he could trust was his father, who had recently retired and moved to the mountains outside of Golden, Colorado.

He left his car and his cell phone and packed a bag. He didn't want to be tracked. He paid cash for a bus ticket and headed out west. The ride was long and boring. Durham didn't seem to notice. He was only concerned with the other passengers. Why were they all on this bus?

When he finally arrived in Golden, he grabbed his canvas duffel bag off of the bus and headed downtown. He pulled out a piece of paper that he had written his father's address on. It was just northwest of town. He began walking. He would take back roads and alleys in an effort to lose anyone that may be following him. After a few hours of walking, he arrived at his father's home. It was a small house away from the city. You could see the flat irons from the back yard. It was gorgeous. Durham was excited to see his father and felt a calm wash over him.

He knocked on the door. It opened to a man that Durham barely recognized.

"Durham?! What are you doing here, my boy?" his father asked excitedly "Come in! What a great surprise!"

His father looked different. *It's happening to him, too!* His father's face was changing, just like his own hands. The nose was stretching and the ears were moving toward the back. The mouth was crooked. He didn't know what to do.

"Dad, it's happening to you, too," Durham exclaimed fearfully.

"What are you talking about? Is everything OK?" His father asked carefully.

"My hands started changing, and then people were

coming after me, and I didn't know what to do and now your face is different too, and I'm afraid and I don't know what to do." He began to sob.

His father hugged him.

"It's OK, Son. Come inside and we will get this figured out.

As they began to walk in, Durham saw a shadow of another person.

"Who else is here?!" he asked frantically. "I just saw them."

"There's no one else here, Durham. Just me."

"I SAW THEM!" He was panicked now.

His father looked at him deeply, with fear and compassion. He had to calm his son down. He had to get him some help. His son was ill.

"Do you want something to drink? I'm going to make a quick phone call. There's plenty in the kitchen. Help yourself."

"Who are you calling?" Durham questioned.

"Just a friend of mine. It'll only take a minute. Relax on the couch. Help yourself to the kitchen. I'll get the spare bedroom ready for you. You're safe here, Son."

His father went to the table and grabbed his phone. He began to dial and walked into the next room.

Durham saw the shadow outside the window again. *What do they want?!* He stood and ran over to look outside. He heard his father talking into the next room. He heard the words, "yes, he's here right now." He was lost. He thought that his father could be trusted, but now he wasn't so sure. There was something different about him. His face had changed. Something wasn't right about any of this. *What do they want? My hands. They're after my hands.*

He was positive now. What else could it be? His father was keeping him there for them to come and take his hands. He had to move.

He grabbed his bag and headed for the door. The sun was still blinding as he ran down the street. He wasn't sure where to go, but he knew it wasn't safe there, and if it wasn't safe at his own father's house, it wasn't safe anywhere. He hadn't slept. He hadn't eaten. That's when Durham ran off to the streets, tired, hungry, and alone.

Get ready for the scare of your life, buddy. He waited just a few more seconds as the bag continued to tug from its chains.

"HANDS IN THE AIR DOCTOR DICKINBALLS!" Durham jumped to his feet and screamed.

There was no robbery. There was no person trying to take his bag. It was just a dog, a labradoodle more specifically, that was pulling at it, almost like he was trying to wake him.

"Oh, it's just a widdle doggy," Durham said. "I'm sorry puppy. I didn't mean to scare you."

He took off the gloves he wore to hide his hands and reached out to pet the dog.

"You're a good boy, aren't you?"

Of course I am.

Durham froze. *Did the dog just speak or was that in my head?*

They sat and stared at each other. Minutes passed. Something felt so good about this dog. There was warmth in its eyes that couldn't be found in the alleys or streets. The dog was telling him something, and he knew what it was. It was a mission. It was the purpose and the answers he had been searching for his entire life. He began to sob uncontrollably before he hugged the labradoodle like a child.

He stood up, threw his gloves in the alley for someone else to use, and he grabbed his things. He knew what he had to do. He had to help Colin Lodestar.

FIFTEEN

It was 1971. BJ adjusted the volume on his record player. He was listening to Sketches of Spain and had a glass of iced tea in his left hand. The ice never melted in Limbo.

He sat on his couch in his Watcher's quarters and looked out of the windows and into the sky. He wondered about Heaven. He imagined harps and reefer. A ringing sound from the corner desk interrupted his daydream.

He walked over and looked through the gazing ball. Colin was just finishing up some chores on the farm. It was an easy gig. Colin never did much to keep BJ on his toes; he just woke up at the same time and did the same chores…every single day. It was pretty boring.

However, on this particular day there was something new in the air. Colin ran inside to clean himself up. He was rebuilding fences for the chickens. He suspected a fox, but they could never seem to catch it.

The shower was quick and efficient, and Colin was looking through his closet for some nice clothes. He was going to go out with some kids from school. It was their senior year, and they were all celebrating their final days as high school students.

BJ almost wished Colin would get into trouble, but he knew better. Colin was a good kid. He got A's and B's in class. He was always respectful and on time. He was a classic beta male. He didn't play any sports in school and was never seen at any social events. He liked to keep to himself and read comic books and write terrible poetry.

> The clouds move gracefully through the sky
> With every shape a product of chance
> Elephants and dogs and pigs that fly
> ...Pants?

Colin's mother was in the kitchen humming along to the radio. His father was still cleaning himself up for dinner. His father had been ill for some time. It was a common argument in the household, that he should visit the doctor. Everyone knew that it wasn't good. What his father knew was that there wasn't much money for the doctor and that a diagnosis would most definitely send them into bankruptcy.

When he finally made the appointment and learned about his stage four colon cancer, Colin blamed his procrastination for the dire news. If he would have gone sooner, maybe there would have been something they could have done.

Dinner was a family favorite: roasted chicken, green beans, and mashed potatoes. Colin's mother sat the meal on the kitchen counter to wait for everyone to join. Colin darted down the stairs and didn't even bother grabbing a plate. He finished his dinner before his mother could tell him to slow down. A car honked outside, and Colin gave a halfhearted, "Have a good night. I'll be back later!" as he rushed past his father, who was more focused on the food than his wayward son.

"Have fun, Son." His father tossed back.

Colin wasn't usually one for a party. He liked to keep to himself. Tonight was different, though. Tonight everyone was heading out to Freakers, including Anna. He was crazy about Anna, and told himself that he was going to get up the nerve to talk with her tonight. He knew deep down that he would probably chicken out; like he had the last fifteen times he had planned on it, but he was determined all the same.

Colin ran outside and jumped into the passenger seat of his best friend, Ben's 1967 Ford Falcon. They backed out of the long farm land driveway and headed into the setting sun. The small vehicle made a pathetic grumble as it took on the gravel roads just outside of town.

Freakers was a common party spot for the local highschoolers. It was a long gravel road in the middle of eighty acres of abandoned farm land. The kids would follow the gravel for a few miles until it met a large creek. There was no bridge and the creek was too deep for any car to drive through, so the kids would stop there and practice drinking and smoking. Partying, like most things, has a learning curve, and Colin threw it off.

The Falcon slid to a stop as dust from the gravel floated away. There was a line of twenty-something cars all pulled over to the side of the road, and a small bonfire glowed in the dusk ahead of them. The sun was nearly set behind the mountains in the distance, and on the east side of the road was a huge field that seemed to go on for miles. The farm that used to occupy the land had been foreclosed many years ago, and what was once a beautiful cattle farm had slowly faded away into a place of wild.

Colin and Ben walked down the gravel road toward the creek. Sounds of a radio could be heard coming through the open windows of a pickup truck. A few kids sat on its open tailgate, sharing a joint.

"Hey guys." Ben said, hiding his awkwardness. They nodded back. Colin waved.

*   *   *   *   *

The bonfire set flickering orange specks into the sky as a skinny, half-drunk kid tossed a log on top of it. Some girls cursed at him as the ashes floated toward their foldable camping chairs. Colin recognized the kid. It was Jonathon Banks.

Jonathon came from a well liked family in the area. He was a friendly guy, who made good grades and had a likeable personality. He was a star basketball player. However, at the moment his motor skills were a bit compromised. He could only let out a giggle as the girls yelled at him.

"DUDES!" his eyes lit up as he saw Colin and Ben walk toward the fire.

"Hey Jonathon, what's up?" Colin asked before being hugged by the tower of an athlete.

Colin laughed a little. All the nerves that he had in coming to the party started to disappear. Someone grabbed a beer from a cooler and tossed to him. He cracked it open and sat on a log near the fire.

More and more kids began to arrive and eventually the creek was alive with the sounds of laughter, car radios, and the occasional tears from someone who had too much to drink. Colin scanned the party occasionally for Anna, but had yet to see her.

"You having fun?" Ben asked as he sat down next to his buddy.

"Yeah, this is great. It's good to get out. The farm has

been keeping me busy," Colin responded.

"You seen Anna yet?" Ben asked.

"No..." Colin said. He took another sip. He was starting to get a little blurry.

"She just got here with Katelyn. You going to finally say something?"

Colin was feeling pretty good, but decided to grab one more beer, for fortune's sake.

"I don't know what to say," he said.

"Just say that you wish you would have told her how gorgeous she is a long time ago. Or something like that. Girls love that stuff."

"Oh...that's good. Thanks man. You know I always loved you," Colin said to his friend. His words were beginning to slur.

"I know buddy. Save it for Anna. Here, have a nip of this." Ben handed him a bottle.

"What's this?"

"Amigo, this is Tequila."

Colin took a slam and stood up. Then he saw her. She walked into the soft glow of the bonfire. She had long brown hair and light blue eyes that glowed orange in the light. She made eye contact with Colin and smiled. He stared back, blankly.

Another person came over and offered them a drink. She laughed and took a bottle that was handed to her. She was with a couple of other girls that Colin recognized from school. They were at a wedding reception beforehand, and Anna was still wearing a dress but had changed into tennis shoes.

They sat opposite one another with the fire between them for a while. Colin was paralyzed by nerve. He didn't know how to approach her and then if he was even successful at that, an ever more difficult task lay beyond:

conversation. He felt doomed.

The night was moving on, and the mosquitoes started biting. The occasional buzz in the ear was mostly drowned out by the buzz from the alcohol, so most of the kids didn't notice them. Anna began swatting at her exposed shins, cursing the bastards back to the Hell they came from. Colin remembered noticing a can of bug spray in Ben's car. This was his chance. He stood up and jogged back up the gravel road.

Colin grabbed the spray and walked back to the fire. Anna was sitting with her back to him. She smacked a bug from her neck.

"Can I spray you?" Colin asked her.

"WHAT?!" She spun around with a sense of confusion.

"I'm sorry! I know how that sounded. I mean...with the bug spray...I saw you were getting bit...Would you like me to spray you with bug spray?"

Anna laughed. "YES PLEASE! These bastards are driving me crazy!"

Colin tried to be gentle as he sprayed the poison onto the back of her neck. She grabbed the can and sprayed her legs and arms.

"Thank you!" she said.

"I do what I can." Colin thought that sounded smoother in his head.

"Sit down." Anna moved over and made room on the fallen tree she was sitting on.

Colin sat down next to her. There was a weird silence.

"I'm surprised to see you out here," she said.

"What? At a party?"

"Yeah."

"I like to party...it's just that by 'party' I mean stay home and read."

She laughed.

"Besides, I figured we're almost done with school. Why not let loose a little bit and see if there's anything else to learn from the high school experience."

"Well..," Anna smiled, "you could learn how to smoke a joint in the woods with a freshly sprayed mountain girl."

"Sounds like a worthy lesson. Lead the way." Colin held his hand out. His heart was pounding.

They walked down a small path toward the edge of the water and lit up. They laughed and talked about future plans now that they were adults. Anna planned on moving to Boulder and going to college. She had a job lined up at the dinner theater. It sounded like an adventure. Colin was jealous. He knew that his path was staying home and taking care of the farm. His father didn't have it in him to work much longer. Colin was torn between animosity and duty.

They sat down on the rocks and tossed pebbles into the rushing stream. Colin was in Heaven; and for the first time in his life he felt a unique confidence. He knew Anna felt something, too. Their connection was certain. He looked at her and felt inspired.

They were interrupted by a commotion from the bonfire back up the path.

"RUN!" someone yelled. The glow from the bonfire went out suddenly.

Colin helped Anna to her feet. They spun around to meet one of Anna's friends stumbling through the pebbles toward them.

"Cops!" she yelled to them.

Colin's heart sank into his stomach. He was in some major trouble.

"Shit! We have to run!" Anna said.

Before they knew it, a herd of high school students

were scrambling toward the creek. The splashes were somewhat muted by the running water as they began to jump in and swim across to the other side. Colin realized that the only way out was to run from the police.

"COME ON!" Anna said. She held out her hand.

"I can't run from the police! My folks will kill me!" Colin argued.

"If I DON'T run from the police my folks will kill me!" Anna said. "Come on! They'll never catch us!"

"I...I can't," Colin said.

"Take my hand, Colin. We will be fine," she said calmly with her hand held toward him.

Take her hand, cat, BJ told him. He didn't want him to be a coward. He knew Colin would regret this.

Flashlights started peering down the path and the sound of the officers' walkie talkies were floating through the surrounding trees.

Don't do it, another voice whispered to him.

"Colin," Anna said with disappointment.

Do it. This is what you want! BJ was standing now. This was his chance!

Anna looked at Colin deeply. Her hand still reaching toward him.

"I can't do it," Colin said shamefully. "We can't run from the cops. What if we get in trouble!?"

One of the boys ran by and grabbed Anna by the shoulders.

"Come on!" the boy said. Anna turned around and dove into the creek. She swam across and looked back at Colin. They caught eyes one more time. She looked disappointed as she turned and ran off with the rest of the party.

The police approached.

"I...uh...I surrender!" Colin said and put his hands

up.

The police walked up to Colin. One officer laughed.

"You can put your hands down, son." He pointed his flashlight around the area.

"We got 'em boys, don't worry. They all took a swim." The rest of the officers chuckled.

"What's your name?"

"Colin Lodestar," Colin replied quietly. He was imagining the food in jail.

"Come on, kid. Let's get you home."

SIXTEEN

It was morning. Dave was drinking coffee sitting at the table across from Jack and the two residents of Limbo. He was the only other one of the band members who was home during the incident, but after two years of living with a pro-party, anti-day job, rock and roll band, he had sound proofed his bedroom, so he heard nothing of a demonic battle or explosion.

"OK, so let me see if I have this straight," Dave began, breaking the silence. He spoke with a gentle southern accent from growing up in a small town in New Mexico.

"This guy here used to be a jazz musician in Chicago and was thrown into an oncoming bus by his twin brother, who was also a jazz musician and who was also killed by the same bus. His brother was a little more evil. I'm guessing from the whole murder-suicide thing, so he went to Hell..."

"Purgatory." BJ interjected.

"Right. Purgatory. So he went to Purgatory and you went to Heaven."

"Limbo," Colin said.

"Limbo. Right. And in Limbo you became this guy's

spirit guide or whatever the hell you want to call it. Then years later, your brother came back up here to earth and murdered the farm kid."

"He stabbed me with a railroad spike," Colin said

"Okay, that's actually pretty bad ass, and we can circle back to that later. So... he kills this guy with a railroad spike. This, in turn, sent him to Limbo, which sent jazzman to Heaven?"

"Well... it sent me to the line to get into Heaven. It's more like a giant waiting room," BJ corrected.

"Okay. Sure, whatever. So you're waiting to get into Heaven and the farm kid becomes Jack's spirit guide or whatever. Which, by the way, Kyle right? You're doing a terrible job."

"Colin," BJ said.

"Sorry. Colin, you're doing a terrible job. Jack is a nightmare. It's a wonder he still has his job. Anyway, Johnny Coltrane over here is waiting for Heaven and enjoying himself, I assume playing harps and shit. Then, in some sort of afterlife conspiracy, a bunch of Hellish demons attacked you guys, and you ran into some caves and in the middle of the struggle you fell into a river that sent you back here to Earth."

"When you put it like that, it sounds kind of out there," Colin said.

"No. Not out there at all. This is all *very* believable, and I *definitely* don't think Jack's fanny pack full of psychedelics has *anything* to do with it." Dave sipped his coffee. "So the twin brother takes over the place and replaces you in line so that he will get into Heaven and do what?"

"Well, I'm guessing that he'll try and let the rest of the demons..." BJ said.

"You know what?" Dave interrupted. "I don't really

care. Let's move forward. So, your twin brother is up there, and you're down here and the farm kid is down here so you guys think, 'hey, we have to find Jack' because he will obviously be *tons* of help. This brings you to our house, where you say that you got into a fist fight with a couple of demons from Hell."

"Purgatory." Jack corrected.

"Right. Purgatory. Demons. From Purgatory. Demons from Purgatory that you threw some of my gasoline on. Which then, SET MY FUCKING TRUCK ON FIRE?!"

"Yeah..." Colin was hesitant to answer. "I didn't know that was going to happen."

"How could you have known that? If it's one thing I've learned over the years, it's that you can never be too sure on what's going to happen in a demon fight."

Dave finished his coffee in one slow gulp. He set his mug down firmly on the table.

"Maybe we should get going..," BJ mentioned.

"So do you guys have a number I can call? Is there someone I can talk to from Purgatory who can pay for my truck? Will Jesus be covering the costs? Because I checked on my auto insurance, and weirdly enough... EXPLODING DEMONS AND HELL-FIRE AREN'T COVERED. NEITHER IS PIXIE SHIT OR GHOUL PISS OR CRACKS IN THE WINDSHIELD FROM HITTING GOBLINS ON THE INTERSTATE!"

"Did you see if it qualifies as an act of God? That's an insurance thing right?" Jack asked. "I mean, it doesn't get more 'act of God' than this, right?"

Dave was not amused as he stared at them.

"We should probably get out of your hair. You just woke up, and I'm sure you've got things to do. Let's get out of here, guys. Jack don't you have to work today?"

Colin said.

"I do. What time is it? Oh Hell! Yep. I am supposed to work in… three minutes ago."

They stood up and hustled toward the door. Jack was first out and ran to his van to start it up.

"WHEN YOU SEE MOSES NEXT, ASK HIM IF HE KNOWS A GOOD UPHOLSTERY GUY! I'M GOING TO BE PARTING SOME RED SEAS AND BEATING SOME ASSES IF MY TRUCK ISN'T REPLACED SOON! YOU'RE GOING TO WISH IT WAS DEMONS AFTER YOU!"

"I don't think he believes us," Colin said as he jumped into the van.

SEVENTEEN

Thousands of demons were lining up outside of the buildings in Purgatory. The ground was cracked and dry. The glows from fiery lava spouting out of geysers lit up the cave like walls in the distance. They had been gathered from all over the many parts of Hell. Being a part of the attacks on Limbo was always a jackpot for the poor souls of Hell. It was like finally getting out of a sauna, that is, if instead of eucalyptus, that sauna was burning with the pain and sorrow of all that is evil in the world.

Amauros glided smoothly across the front of the small army being put together. There was barely a bounce in his gate. Things were going perfectly. The Rocky Mountain Division was out of commission. BJ and Colin were back on Earth and not in any position to be a problem for the time being. Chrissy was in his position outside the waiting room, and in 14 hours he would be taking his brother's place as he entered the pearly gates. Once inside, there was very little standing between Amauros' army and infiltrating their entrance of Heaven. This would be the first time in history that a Duke of Hell has been able to wage an attack on Heaven itself. If the attack is successful they would be able to hold a position and take control of the Rocky Mountain Division. This would give them a direct route to Heaven and give Purgatory free reign over the Rocky Mountains. Souls would be pouring into Hell faster than ever. Amauros could already taste the power he was about to wield.

"We're almost ready to begin marching toward Limbo, sir." One of the demonic generals reported to the duke.

"How many soldiers do we have?" Amauros responded.

"Forty-thousand for the first wave. More are still arriving for the second," the general answered.

"We head to the caves in one hour."

Amauros walked toward the doors of Purgatory. He had one more thing to do before leading his army into Limbo. BJ and Colin had escaped twice now, and with them still free they posed a threat to his plan.

The halls were quiet as he strolled through them. He approached a cubicle to his left and stood at the entrance. One of the demons was in his chair with his headset on watching the screen on his desk.

"Where are they?" Amauros asked the demon.

"Aye, the mangy land lovers are in Jack's vessel heading toward his job at the corporate watering hole, Pepper's… right smartly if you ask me. No regard for the common laws of the road. They narrowly escaped the two that were sent after them," The demon answered.

Ever since the Watchers fell back to Earth, Amauros has been working closely with Seven Fingers Johnson, who had been assigned as Jack's pusher. Seven Fingers had been in Purgatory for a long time, and was very good at his job. He had died at sea back in 1695, and for all of this time in Purgatory, he had never once spoken with the boss until recently.

"We need a different approach." Amauros thought aloud. "Going after Colin and BJ is pointless. We need to focus on the weak one of the group. Tell me about Jack."

"Oh, Jack Charlton be a fierce one. He loves his grog and is a mighty fine poet. That there satchel he wears on his front is where he keeps his loot. Magic treats. Aye, I be known to splice the main brace e'ry now an' then. So I can't blame a man for imbibing."

The dead sailor continued softly.

"'Twas a beauty that did ol' Jack wrong. You can't trust the lassies. Which is why ol' Seven-Fingers Johnson stayed single me whole life. Aye, there's a few nights I'd crack Jenny's tea cup, if you know what I mean, but the sea was me only true love."

Amauros perked at this information.

"A beauty? A girl? Who was it?" He asked.

"Well that be, Olivia. Jack was right fond of her, but she was quite a strumpet, that one. Ol' Jack got done wrong. The lassies just can't be trusted. That's why the sea was me only true love."

"That's it! Tell me what you know about Olivia."

"Oh, Olivia be a fine looking lass. She has long slender legs, dark brown hair, eyes as blue as the sea, which was me only true love, ya know. You just can't trust the lassies these days."

"Who is her pusher?"

"Oh…that be Jared. He's a bilge-sucking scallywag, that Jared. Nose as brown as a berry."

Amauros walked away from the grumbling pirate without even a goodbye. He had to find Jared. Olivia was the perfect weapon to use against Jack and his new Watcher friends.

"Aye, hoist the mizzen me hearty!" Seven-Fingers

cheerfully encouraged Amauros as he walked away. *Don't bother saying 'thank you' either you dick* he thought as he turned back to his desk.

*　　　*　　　*　　　*　　　*

The demons were patrolling the halls of Limbo as Chrissy approached the doors to the waiting room. The waiting room was connected to all of the different divisions of Limbo, which were all still up and running and clueless as to the takeover in the Rocky Mountain Division. A giant demonic wolf-man would be a big red flag if he were to just walk in, so he was waiting for his human form to return. In about 14 hours, his brother's wait would be over and he would be allowed into Heaven.

He was already starting to change back to his original form. It was a strange feeling seeing himself closer and closer to the underappreciated saxophone player that he once was. He felt smarter, and less like a drooling beast. In just a little more time, he would walk into the waiting room and take his brother's place. The rest of the demons would make their escape, and no one would be the wiser.

*　　　*　　　*　　　*　　　*

Olivia was on the couch, binge-watching The Gilmore Girls. She was bored, and her new boyfriend was no help. The couch was warm beneath the sun shining through her curtains. She was wearing an old t shirt and her favorite pair of 'comfy shorts' and had long forgotten that they once belonged to Jack. She did her best to avoid thinking of Jack. It always came with a slight pang of guilt and a heavy pang of annoyance.

Olivia was from a small town out east, and had never gone out on her own before packing up and moving to Denver. She wanted some excitement, and maybe that's what she found in Jack. He may not have the kind of stability she wanted in a man, but he had all the adventure a man wanted in himself. She spent years with him, and it was the most romantic time of her life, but she couldn't handle the fear of what the future would hold if she were to stay with a man like Jack. The music and the travelling were constant, and a steady job was nowhere in sight. It was in a moment of weakness, while out with her friends, she met what would be her new boyfriend, and she cheated on Jack. It wasn't premeditated. She never meant to hurt him, but it was too late now, and she was determined to prove her choices were the right ones.

She knew deep down that she at least owed him an apology, and one day she swore she would give it to him. Not today, though. Not with the Gilmore Girls on.

Get up. Something came over her. She felt different.

She got up from the couch and went to wash her face in the bathroom. The lights slowly brightened as she looked at herself in the mirror.

Lookout Mountain. A memory flashed into her mind of the time she and Jack went out to Lookout Mountain and saw Buffalo Bill's grave. It was a good memory and one that they both held dear. They were both new to the area and a shared excitement in exploring a new home is a bond that is hard to break.

Apologize to Jack. She felt a need to reach out to him. It was hard to explain why it was so compelling, but she knew she had to do it. She would sleep better at night if she could make things right with him. She needed to do it on the mountain, on the trails to where they used to walk and talk about everything. That would be a perfect way to make amends. She was going to invite him to Lookout Mountain and apologize over some wine and a snack. Jack was never big on snacks; he always just wanted to eat meat.

Wine and crackers will have to be good enough.

She went into the bedroom and got dressed. He was probably at work, so she could swing into Pepper's on the way to the store. There was a wave of excitement. Almost like fate guiding her along.

*   *   *   *   *

Amauros was standing over Jared's back as the demon was pushing Olivia to apologize to Jack.

"Excellent work, Jared," Amauros said to his minion.

"Anything for the team," Jared responded. His glasses were missing an earpiece and were crooked on his nose.

Amauros left the suck-up's cubicle and began walking outside toward his army. It was almost time to head to the caves and prepare to march on to Limbo. He pulled five demons to the side.

"I have a special mission for you," he said to the eager creatures. "It's risky, and you must not be seen. I need you to go to the trails on the top of Lookout Mountain and wait for Jack Charlton to show up with his two Watcher friends. I want you to capture the Watchers."

"What do you want us to do with the living one?" one of the demons asked.

"I don't care. Kill him. Have fun with it."

EIGHTEEN

BJ and Colin were drinking a giant glass of beer while Jack worked away behind the bar at Pepper's. It was a strange thing, to be serving a beer to your Watcher. It was a strange thing, as well, to be serving a beer to your Watcher's Watcher. Then, add the strangeness of bartending after a couple of demons blew up your fiddle player's truck. However, Jack grew mushrooms in a fanny pack. He wasn't just used to strange. He embraced it.

The lunch rush was about to begin and Jack was furiously getting his bar organized and ready.

"So what the heck are we supposed to do now?" Colin asked BJ.

"I'm just as lost as you, cat," BJ responded. He took a sip from his 23 ounce beer. "I love the wine in Limbo, but I sure did miss a cold beer."

Colin agreed. Now that they were with Jack and he was okay, they had a minute to sit and figure out their next move.

"We somehow need to get back to Limbo. What happens if we die? Maybe we could go jump in front of a bus or something."

BJ did not like that idea.

"No bus, my man." He took a drink from his glass. "I don't think killing ourselves will help us. Here's the way I see it. We can't get back through the caves. We know that. But..."

BJ leaned in closer. Colin listened.

"Obviously, everyone around us has somebody watching us from back, home right? So, in theory, all we have to do is talk to any random stranger and then their Watcher will see it and hear us and somehow be able to get us a message and tell us how to get back up there, right?"

Colin sipped his beer and nodded in agreement.

"So, why hasn't anyone helped us yet? Who was watching over that guy that brought us to Jack's? He just picked up two random strangers hitch-hiking? We don't even have shoes on, man. That's not safe. What if we were murderers?! Someone should have been watching over that dude. Look around. We're in a bar right now with forty people around us."

BJ turned around and grabbed the adjacent bar patron by the shoulders. It was a skinny young Latina woman with fear in her eyes as a big burly man dressed in clothes from the fifties began to shake her as if waking her up.

"HELLO! Can you hear us up there? We could use a hand!" BJ yelled at her.

Jack ran over to the bar and smacked BJ's arms away from the woman.

"I'm sorry, ma'am, these guys are a little..." he pantomimed drinking as he hinted at the two Watchers. He then turned to the guys.

"What the hell are you guys doing? Knock it off, man. This is my job! Which, yeah I don't actually care about when I think about it, but still...be cool," Jack angrily whispered before returning back to work.

BJ turned back to Colin.

"So this means that something isn't right. Limbo is out of commission, my ivory brother."

"So what now?" Colin asked.

"We need to head to another Division. Maybe they haven't gotten to any other areas yet."

"What's the next closest Division?"

"Nevada? Sin City Division."

"So we head to Nevada and talk to the first person we see?"

"Yeah. Unless there's a better idea?" BJ was thinking aloud "Should we take Jack's van?"

Colin thought about this. He didn't want to make Jack's life more difficult than Jack was already making it on himself, but he knew that they were in a serious dilemma. He was still obligated to keep watch over Jack. Without him here, who knows what the pushers would be making him do. The pushers would have free reign.

"BJ..," Colin said, "if Limbo is out of service, then that means that the pushers have no opposition."

"It'll be chaos. We should probably get out of town sooner than later."

"Okay, well we need to take Jack with us...so one more beer while we wait?"

"Yep."

They ordered another round from Jack. He was pouring the beers when his attention shifted to the door, as Olivia walked through. *What the hell is SHE doing here?* His thoughts were interrupted by the beer flowing over the glass. He wiped the foam away and quickly did his best to pretend he didn't notice her as she approached the bar.

"Hi Jack," she said meekly.

"Olivia?" Jack turned to her and acted surprised. "What are you doing out during the day? Aren't you worried that you'll turn to stone?" He asked innocently.

She ignored the insult.

"I was hoping to talk to you for a minute," she asked

"Oh sure, but bear with me. We haven't talked in a while, and my Parseltongue is a little rusty."

"Oh, I'm sure you don't need a translator for some of the words I'd like to say to you..!" She started to get angry. She hated when he made fun of Harry Potter.

Calm down and remember why you're here. The thoughts came into her head like an outside voice. *Just ask him to meet you after he gets off of work.*

"Look..." she said as she collected herself "I know things have been hectic so I'm here to make a truce of some sort. I was hoping you'd meet me after work for a little picnic, and we can make amends."

Jack was taken aback.

"Uh...what?" he couldn't believe what he was hearing. "You want to have a picnic? Is this a trick?" He was suspicious.

"No trick. Just being an adult. Let's meet at the trails on Lookout Mountain and talk, almost like old times. What time are you off?"

"2:30," He answered. He stood there bewildered. All the anger had faded. "Just like old times?"

"*Almost* like old times. I'll see you around three," she said before she turned around and walked out the door.

Colin stared in disbelief. *It's starting.*

Chaos.

*   *   *   *   *

Catfish was walking down a sidewalk. He passed a

corner on Wadsworth and 18th and was heading north. The late morning sun was shining on his face. He felt like a new man on his mission. Suddenly, he felt a shift in the wind. *West.*

"I hear you," he said to no one. He looked to the western sky toward the mountains. He started toward Lookout Mountain.

NINETEEN

"Jack, are you insane?!" Colin yelled into the back of Jack's van through its open rear doors.

They were in the parking lot of Pepper's, and Jack was cleaning out the van and folding the seats into a bed. The occasional beer can clanked into the parking lot as he rearranged the garbage into random bags and containers.

"What are you talking about? This is what I've been waiting for. An apology from Olivia! That's a rare frigging gem, my friend," Jack questioned back.

"You don't think that this is all kind of convenient?" Colin asked.

BJ had found the remnants of what appeared to be a joint under the front seat. He lit it up and coughed as he joined the conversation.

"You gotta admit the timing is crazy, cat."

"Yeah, we can't go meet Olivia right now. We have to get out of town as soon as possible!"

"Well, hop in your car and head out. Have a safe, oh wait..," Jack said sarcastically. "You don't have a car, because you're 'ghosts.' Better start counting bricks then, Swayze."

He started pulling a sleeping bag out of the middle

section.

"Wait...are we ghosts?" Colin asked BJ.

"I guess so? I haven't really thought about that." BJ responded.

"That's weird. It's not like we're invisible or anything. I just drank a couple beers. It didn't fall through me and onto the floor or anything," Colin said.

"Yeah...I don't know, cat. We're dead, though."

"You could be zombies?" Jack shrugged.

"No. Zombies have a whole set of specifics and, like, a canon to follow. We aren't wandering around looking for brains to munch on," Colin said.

"That's true," BJ nodded. "I ain't hungry for no brains."

"I don't know. It doesn't matter right now. We can circle back to this later."

"Well now you've got me thinking..," BJ continued and relit the joint he found.

Colin started pacing.

"Jack, you can't trust Olivia." Colin kicked at the ground in frustration. "The timing is just too weird."

"You don't even know her!" Jack began to raise his voice.

"I've seen what she has done to you. Look, I know deep down, Olivia is probably a fantastic person. In fact, I would love for you to work things out with her. I would. She was great for you, but this is crazy. We need to leave town before it gets bad," Colin pleaded.

"What's crazy is that I actually let you random dudes come with me to work this morning. I mean, all the crap about being ghosts made perfect sense when I was tripping, but I'm still not completely sold. So if you'll excuse me, I need to finish putting this bed together so I have a place to lay my lady down once we make amends…"

Colin was flustered. He began pacing back and forth as Jack rearranged his van into the love machine it used to be.

"I get it. This is weird to just accept. We are basically strangers to you," Colin began. "But I know you, man. I've been watching over you all your life. I know that in high school, you were the athlete of the month, and you made hundreds of photocopies of your picture from the newspaper so that you could autograph them and give them to people as Christmas gifts."

"Public knowledge; I gave hundreds of those out." Jack responded from the van's interior.

"I know that you love the movie You've Got Mail, and you watch it drunk and alone, late at night."

"Everyone loves that movie. Tom Hanks and Meg Ryan had a natural chemistry! Do I need to mention Sleepless in Seattle? Joe Versus the Volcano?!"

"I know that you moved a lot, as a kid. I know that you love to fish but hate to touch the worms. I know that when you were twelve you had a crush on Amy, the girl who lived up the street from you. When you finally worked up the courage to go tell her, she laughed in your face and told all of her friends. I remember watching you crying in the trees behind your house."

Jack stepped out of the back of the van.

"How could you know that? Who the hell are you?" Jack's eyes were big.

The sounds of broken glass interrupted them. A car had just rear ended an SUV at a red light on the street adjacent to the parking lot. The driver of the SUV was a young girl. She immediately got out of her car, and in a rage ran to the car behind her, opened the door and pulled out a fifty year old man. They began yelling at each other until the woman punched the man in the stomach and began beating him.

The drivers of the cars around them began to get out, with what looked to be, the intention of breaking it up until it erupted into an all out brawl. Sirens could be heard in the distance.

The three looked in shock.

"Chaos," Colin reiterated.

"Okay, fine. I'll believe you," Jack said. "But if it's about to get as bad as you say it is, then we're taking Olivia with us."

They jumped into the van and left the parking lot.

"Works for me," BJ said as he jumped into the front seat.

"What? We need to GO!" Colin panicked.

"It's the right thing to do, cat."

*   *   *   *   *

The mountains towered in the distance as the three cruised west on Highway 6. It was mid-afternoon with perfect sunshine. The van was quiet. Jack turned the radio on and began scanning the stations, looking for nothing in particular.

They passed the exit for I-70 and began to curve around the outskirts of Golden, Colorado. It was a beautiful little town tucked away just west of Denver. As they continued forward they could see Lookout Mountain ahead of them.

The mountain had a special place in Jack's heart. Olivia and he would spend many afternoons and evenings there, even a night or two in the back of the van. They would hike on the trails and picnic on the top. They would sit on an old rock that resembled a couch and smoke a hookah as the sun set. Jack would make fun of the bicyclists on their way up to the top of the mountain, and Olivia would laugh. Jack always figured that he would propose to her on that mountain. They were young and in love. Life was golden.

Life, though, is life. Sometimes, love falls down and doesn't get back up. Maybe that's what really hurts. We grow up with the idea that love never gives up. Love is all you need. That isn't always true.

Life is funny. Jack was thinking about his situation, on the way to Lookout Mountain wearing a black polo shirt bearing the cheesy logo of a corporate restaurant. He's broke. He's apparently responsible for blowing up his fiddle player's truck. He was joined by two apparent dead guys and about to meet with a woman that he can't figure out if he loves or hates.

They turned left onto 19th Street and began up the foothills. As they progressed up the curvy roads, the sun began to set lower on the horizon. Olivia was waiting by her car as they pulled to the side of the road behind it. She was holding a small bag and a bottle of wine. She waved as the van pulled over on to the side of the road. Jack jumped out and ran toward her.

Colin couldn't help but feel happy for Jack, all things considered.

* * * * *

"I see you haven't changed your clothes since work." Olivia laughed as Jack approached her. He had a panicked look in his eyes.

"Olivia, you have to come with me. It's important. We have to leave now!" Jack pleaded as he began to grab the wine and snacks from her.

"Wait…what are you talking about? I just wanted to take a walk and talk a bit. It won't take much time."

"No time, seriously." Jack was always flustered around her since the break up. "There're demons somewhere and people in Limbo aren't working right so people are being mean to each other and hurting each other and it's absolute chaos. The dead guys in the van will help explain!"

"Dead guys in the van?" Olivia couldn't believe her ears. She stepped back.

"Yes…er no I mean. Well, two of them. BJ and Colin. I mean it's not like there are dead bodies in there…well technically I guess, but they're also alive. Like zombies…but not the horror movie kind. No no wait… not like zombies. We decided against that. Colin is like my guardian angel. At first I didn't believe him, but he knows I hate worms. Come on. let's go." He grabbed for her arm to bring her.

"You have two dead people in your van?!" She pulled away. *Is he on drugs?* Olivia was frustrated. This was supposed to be her moment to make amends.

"It's not like I killed anybody… they're fine. I mean… just please come with me and I can explain on the road. We need to get out of Colorado!"

"DAMMIT JACK!" she yelled.

*   *   *   *   *

"I don't think it's going so well," Colin said, as the two of them watched from the middle section of the van.

"This is kind of a tough sell," BJ responded.

They both fell out of their bucket seats when they felt the crash. The side of the van began denting inwards toward them from some force on the outside. BJ screamed as the van began to flip over. Glass shattered like little mini explosions of reflective light.

*   *   *   *   *

Jack and Olivia watched, frozen in fear and disbelief, as the demons began attacking the van.

Outside, five demons were on the van turning it on its side. They began to smash in the doors with their fists. Two of the demons ripped a spruce tree from the ground and began using it as a hammer to smash the front section of the van in. The doors were all blocked. Colin jiggled the door handle, desperate to escape. The 1998 Ford Econoline had become an outdated, gas-guzzling tomb for the Watchers. They were trapped.

"We gotta go!" Jack exclaimed as he grabbed Olivia and they turned toward the trails into the mountain.

"What should we do about those two?" One of the creatures asked the demon that was standing on top of the van?

"Amauros said to have fun…" she replied. Three of the demons began to pursue the ex lovers.

The thin, brown dirt trail was easy to see against the brush and trees that surrounded it. They were running in a single file line, and losing light as the sun got closer to falling behind the mountains in the distance.

There was no time to stop and think, but Olivia couldn't help the fleeting thoughts in her mind. *He was telling the truth. He wasn't tripping balls. We are being chased by monsters. I never should have contacted Jack. Mom was right.*

Jack was behind Olivia. They were running for their lives. He had some thoughts too, as he stared at her butt in the dimming light. *If we survive this I am SO getting laid.*

Jack looked behind them and saw the furious red glow

of the demons in the dusk behind them.

"They're behind us!" Jack yelled to Olivia.

"We're never going to lose them if we stay on the trail!" she decided. Olivia was always very decisive. Jack had always dug that about her.

They turned off the trail and ran into the woods. The trees began to thin as they came into a clearing. They could hear the demons behind them, screeching and laughing in the distance. They could see the road to their right, which meant they were close to the edge of the mountain. A radio tower sat one hundred yards ahead of them, uphill.

Before they could decide which direction to head they were being surrounded. A demon leapt into the clearing in front of them. He was halfway between them and the tower. Behind them, the other two walked out of the trees. They slowly began toward them.

"Don't bother running. There's nowhere to go but down…" one of the demons chuckled.

TWENTY

"Mr. Charlton, here are the keys to your brand new, used 1998 Ford Econoline."

A man in a white shirt and a green tie handed Jack a key that was attached to a paperclip. Jack grabbed the key and walked outside to his purchase. He was nineteen years old and it was the first automobile he bought on his own. To him it represented his commitment to moving away and starting a band. How else does one begin a journey into the heart of rock and roll? He bought a van.

As the years poured by, the van became a companion to Jack. He had spent many nights sleeping in the folded down back seat. When completely folded out, the backseat was nearly the size of a full size mattress. It had a small TV and VCR built into a wooden frame between the two front seats, which was very luxurious at one time. However, nowadays, it meant that movies on the road were often limited to whatever the band could find on VHS. A few arguments on whether to watch Space Jam or Kazaam, had occurred, which was also the closest thing to a sports argument that the band had ever been in. Jack also had a double VHS version of Titanic, but he kept that to himself. There had been many blurry nights in that van, shared with many "After-show Ashley's." Jack loved that blue Ford Econoline.

He never would have guessed that both he and his van would be killed on the same day.

*   *   *   *   *

BJ and Colin tumbled as the vehicle tipped over. They landed on their backs against the side door. They could feel the vehicle being pushed across the ground. It came to a sudden stop as the back doors were placed flush against a tree. Glass shattered from the front as the demons began pounding in the front doors. They were trapped inside with no way of escaping. They could hear the demons laughing from outside of the van.

"Trapped, boys?" a demon laughed from the outside. "We'll help you out of here just as soon as we're done with your friends out there."

"What the hell are we going to do now, cat?" BJ whispered.

Colin didn't have an answer. His leg was pinned between the bucket seat and the wall of the van below him. BJ maneuvered over to him and help pry his leg out. He kicked a broken TV out of the way and pulled Colin out.

"Sweet beans and rice, this day can suck a butt," Colin whimpered.

"I've been wanting to talk with you about your phrases," BJ whispered.

They could hear the demons begin to scamper around outside, like evil cats in an annoying upstairs neighbor's apartment. Stupid. Pointless. Cats.

Then they heard the sounds of a struggle outside the

van. Something was attacking the demons. WHOOSH. They could hear the sound of a flame engulfing something. It reminded Colin of when he was a kid, and his father lit the grill. He'd give anything to be at a BBQ at the moment, and done with the weight of the afterworld weighing upon him.

WHOOSH. More ignitions, this time with a Hellish scream. Then silence.

*   *   *   *   *

"Olivia, I'm going to distract them and you run." Jack whispered.

She was frozen in fear as the demons approached them. They were jet black, with glowing red embers scattered over them. They resembled a walking piece of burning charcoal. She could smell the sulfur. *How did I get here?!* If she had more time to think, she would have most definitely figured out a way to blame Jack for this predicament. Poor Jack.

"Olivia!" he said again, in a serious tone. "I'm going to charge them. You run back the way we came and get to your car."

"Charge them?!" Olivia said. "Look at them! They're…monsters!"

"And they're about to taste the senseless rage of a hungry and unappreciated artist!"

"Jack, you can't beat them. They'll kill you!"

"Maybe… but I don't know what else to do." Jack looked at her. "I love you, Olivia. I never stopped. I'm sorry for all the stupid arguments. I was scared because I knew that I would never get it right again…like I did with you."

Olivia was frozen in her tracks. "Jack, don't do this…"

She began to cry.

"RUN DAMMIT!"

In an instant Jack was off and heading right toward the one in front. His screams took the demon aback. *What the hell was he doing?* As the songwriter got closer he prepared to swing the bottle of wine he was still holding. In one fell move, the demon backhanded Jack and sent him tumbling across the field. It was a noble attempt, but come on. They're badass creatures from Hell.

The demons laughed as the leader of the three walked over and picked Jack up by the neck. He began to carry him toward the edge of the field and the side of the mountain. His legs were dangling. He was still dazed from the backhanded slap.

Olivia couldn't bring herself to keep running and turned back around to see what was happening.

"NO! JACK!" she pleaded. He distracted them so she could escape. He had saved her life. Now they were going to kill him.

*   *   *   *   *

The Watchers sat silently in their sideways prison of a van. The demons had been silenced for a few minutes. Something was going on out there. Just as BJ was going to attempt to peek through what remained of the front of the van window, the rear windows were smashed open. A dirty older man peeked through.

"Colin?" he asked.

"Yeah…" Colin answered with a confused look on his face.

"My friends call me Catfish," he answered and reached his hand into the van. "I was sent here to help you."

Colin reached forward as the man helped him slide out

of the broken window. He dusted himself off as he stood up and noticed the scorch marks on the road next to him. They were the same marks that were left when he threw gasoline on the creatures at Jack's house. He looked over at Catfish as he was pulling the burly, black piano player from the vehicle.

The older man was wearing ragged clothes. A brown pair of pants and a down winter coat with holes in the elbows. He hadn't been bathed in a long time, and you could feel the dreadlocks forming in his matted hair. The cracks in his face were exaggerated from the dirt that covered it. His eyes were blue and piercing. He had no shame of his appearance. His confidence in his purpose was comforting to Colin. He had a good feeling being around Catfish.

He handed Colin a torch made from a broom handle. It was still glowing red-hot.

"Fight fire with fire, right?" He smiled as he grabbed another torch for himself.

"Come on, we have to hurry and find Jack before it's too late," the vagabond said. "They went down these trails. Let's go!"

How does he know Jack? Who the hell is this guy?

The sun was setting as the three men ran into the woods.

*   *   *   *   *

The trail was dark as they forged through, looking for their friend, Jack Charlton and his harpy of an ex-girlfriend, Olivia. Colin still held a grudge.

"You said you were sent to help?" Colin asked their homeless savior.

"Yes. I can help you get back," Catfish Durham

responded.

"How? Who sent you? Who are you?"

"Caves. A dog. Catfish Durham. I already told you that."

"A dog?"

"A labrodoodle. That's how he came to me."

"I don't understand. Would it kill you to embellish a little?!"

They were interrupted by a woman's cries for help ahead of them.

"NO! JACK!"

It was Olivia. They group began to run ahead toward the cries for help. Colin prayed that they weren't too late. They came through the trees to a field and saw Olivia staring out ahead. Colin ran up to her.

"They have him!" she said. She was in shock.

"BJ, will you help her?" Colin insisted.

BJ helped her back to the cover of the trees. Colin and Catfish ran up the field with their torches. The three demons looked toward the two as they approached. One of them was dangling Jack by the neck. He was struggling to breathe as he kicked his legs and tried desperately to release the hold the creature had on him.

"Put him down!" Colin yelled.

The two other demons ran toward them. One of them was fixed on Colin. The Watcher froze, unsure of what to do as the demon began closing in on him. Catfish sprung into action, and like a man possessed maneuvered the monster's weight against him and tossed him to the ground. As the creature began to get back up, the homeless man barreled toward him and swung his torch like a baseball bat, striking the monster in the back of the head. The burning embers from the torch set the creature ablaze and in a blinding flash of the light the demon was gone. The second demon kicked him in the back and sent him to the ground. She was smaller, but faster than the first. Catfish rolled forward from the kick and sat up in time to throw the torch into the creature's stomach, doubling her over and engulfing her in flames. She was gone.

"I guess I'm outnumbered," the remaining demon growled. He was still holding Jack. "We were going to tear this guy's limbs off, but I guess there's no time for that now."

"Put him down, you fiend!" Catfish demanded.

"I guess I'm out matched here." The demon laughed. "What should I do with him?"

Colin saw as Jack tried to say something in protest. The creature wound his arms and with a similar motion of throwing a Frisbee, tossed a helpless Jack into the air, and over the side of the mountain. He could hear Olivia screaming behind them as they watched in horror. Jack's arms were reaching for anything as he flew through the air. He made brief eye contact with Colin before falling out of sight behind the edge of the field.

Colin froze as Catfish grabbed his torch and charged the last remaining demon. He didn't even notice the flash of light as the homeless man sent the creature back to where he came. He only had his thoughts, and they were frozen in time. Everything felt distant. Colin knew that no one could survive the kind of fall that Jack had just taken. He didn't join the others as they ran to the edge of the field, desperate for any sign of life. He didn't have the energy to join in with the tears and sobs. He could only stand there knowing the terrible reality. His client, his friend, and a man that he had been watching over for his entire life, was dead. Colin had failed him, and with Limbo out of service, there was no way he had made it in.

Colin knew there was only one place that Jack could have gone.

Jack Charlton had gone to Hell.

PART 2

"It's a parable. Cute. Let's go eat."
-Christopher Moore

TWENTY-ONE

An empty fish tank in your living room is about as useful as a fork in soup. God felt the same way about the universe. Heaven and Hell had been created so long ago, that God, himself, had easily grown bored with it.

Engineering the universe was a labor of love. Which is a godly way of saying: it was a pain in the ass and didn't pay off much. There were so many issues to work out and then once people got involved it was like herding cats. This is actually why the Lord created cats. It was a passive aggressive revenge of sorts.

Why am I doing all of this? The Lord would think to himself. *These people don't listen.*

The creation process was usually pretty similar each time. First of all, like all of the other worlds he built, there needed to be some sort of order. Balance was the key to creating an interesting world. He had built a couple worlds before Earth that were okay. One of the first worlds he had built was a place that was pure and simple and righteous. It was great at first, but there was no drama or excitement. In an effort to balance this out, he created another place that was the opposite. It was cold and full of dread and darkness. Again, it grew boring.

Creation, like most things, was best perfected by trial and error. So what began as a dark void of infinite possibility became Heaven and Hell, and then, in a stroke of genius BAM...the Lord created balance. You're welcome.

Next up, the Lord picked out a big, empty, rock hurtling through space. God thought to himself, "This could be a fun world full of love and ambition. I could use this place to build creatures that have the same kind of love in their hearts as me. This could work..." Then BAM...Earth, oceans, veggies and all. You're welcome.

Without an anchor, this newborn world would just float around the ever-growing fabric of the universe. This felt unfair to all of the people that would inhabit this world, though. They deserved a home in the universe, not to be some sort of interstellar hobo without a common sky throughout their lives. So the Lord placed this giant rock near one of his favorite stars and let it slowly circle it. However, during the move he accidentally smacked it against some debris and part of it split off. It ended up circling the rock and reflected the light of the star back onto to it, giving parts of the world a beautiful, yet somber glow. God was pleasantly surprised with this and left it. He had a good feeling about it all, and before he stopped creating for the moment, he tossed some stars around and smiled. BAM...the sun and the moon and the stars were there...you're welcome.

God came back after a while and took a look at this world. It was awesome. He was super psyched about how well it all turned out and figured he would shake it up a bit. He was looking down from Heaven when one of his favorite angels came up to him.

"Gabriel, what do you think of this place?" the Lord

asked.

"Looking good, Big Guns. What are you going to do next?"

"Huge fucking lizards, dude."

Gabriel nodded in agreement. "Nice."

That would be pretty bad ass. So the Lord headed down to Earth and began his effort in populating the world with these giant lizards. He loved them. Life on Earth was good for a while, and it looked like the Lord had found a place that he could put all of his love and joy into. BAM dinosaurs...you're welcome.

It was morning time when Big Guns noticed someone walking through the forest on his new world. He looked down from his throne in Heaven and noticed the leaves disintegrating as the figure strolled through.

Son of a bitch! He thought to himself. He stood up from his throne and ran outside onto the golden roads of Heaven. He knew exactly who it was: Lucifer, the asshole. He was just trying to get under his skin. God knew better, but he hated seeing his new world being soiled by that dick head.

"LUCIFER!" the Lord bellowed from on high.

The man stopped for a moment and then walked into a clearing and looked to the sky.

"Yes, mother?" he said, feigning innocence. He was wearing a black robe and had long blond hair.

"Is there a reason you are here? No one is allowed on this new world."

"Well, I just wanted to see what all the fuss was about. I heard you had these beautiful new creatures up here. I only wanted to see them."

"You need to leave, Satan."

Lucifer hated that name, Satan. It just felt mean rolling off the tongue. At that Lucifer looked up and responded, "Of course."

He bowed his head and began to walk away. After a few steps he stopped, looked up to the sky with a terrible smile before spitting on the ground, and making an X in the dirt with his foot. He then continued on his journey.

That night, there was a terrible storm on earth. The Lord was watching as his creatures were scurrying around seeking shelter from the plentiful world they lived in. God knew that this was somehow Lucifer's doing, but decided to see how it played out. Out of nowhere, the sky split and a giant meteorite flew through the atmosphere and crashed right into the very same spot that Lucifer had made an X in the ground.

The sky was covered in debris and the light couldn't shine through. The Lord watched with rage as many of his creatures died. Although, some of them survived and began to adapt to the new world around them, many of them would never be seen again. He knew that Lucifer wanted to be in control, and he was worried that he may have to banish that fucker once and for all. He knew what he had to do next.

He would create creatures that could act as currency. Spiritual economics was the only way to defeat this evil butthole. It was a new concept in the world. He would create souls. All of the beauty and love and joy would be there for the picking, but it was up to these new creations to wade through the glutton and jealousy and fear that would hold them back. This would be the perfect creation. Something that the Lord could love regardless of fault or failure: people. So then BAM... he created people and placed them in the Garden of Eden. You're welcome.

And the Lord loved them in a perfect way.

As time progressed, the battle for souls became more

and more intense and both sides became very invested in the spiritual war. Gabriel was given control over the angelic army. Over time, the war escalated and God had one more thing to create: a doorway between worlds. He knew that eventually the war would have to be fought on the very grounds that he had created, so he sent his son, Jesus, to earth.

What happened in those days was mostly lost in translation. People were easily corrupted and prone to distorting the truth for their own means (especially when it comes to forgiveness, helping the less fortunate, and just generally being cool.) A lot of JC's story was edited and rearranged to serve the powerful and help further their agendas. In fact, thirty years of Jesus' life was completely omitted. No one even acknowledged his childhood comrade, Biff, but that's a story in its own.

After Jesus was betrayed and killed, his body was taken to a tomb. History tells us that his followers denied being on Team Jesus and that they got away without being brutally beaten and murdered like their patriarch. Then, days after his body being entombed, something happened. All of a sudden every disciple who followed Jesus went public with their allegiance, and were thus brutally beaten and murdered. What could make someone change their mind and walk right into the lion's den like that? Well, Jesus came back to life and made them eat some proverbial crow.

Jesus and his dad were looking down from Heaven after his death.

"Well, crap, looks like I'm gonna have to go back down there," Jesus said.

"Yep. Man, I really thought all of those miracles and sermons would have stuck," God responded.

"I know! Remember the sermon on the rock? That

crowd was going wild! I really thought that we had some serious momentum."

"Yeah, they were. I really don't know what went wrong."

"What about the guy that they brought in through the roof? Remember that? Dude was paralyzed! The house was so packed full of people that they couldn't fit him in! They had to lift him down with a bunch of ropes and when I saw him I was like 'walk much?' then BAM I smacked him in the ass and he got up and started PARTYING! What more do these people want?!"

"I know it."

"I walked on water for my sake!"

"I know it."

"Wine anyone?"

"I know it."

"I won't even talk about the whole 'brutally beaten and murdered' thing. That really sucked."

"I know it."

"I have holes in my hands now. Do you know how frustrating it is to shampoo these luscious locks of hair?"

"I can imagine."

"I have to go back down there?"

"Yep. You're going to have to go back down there."

"UGH! Pops, I spent 30 years with those ungrateful fucks. Can't I take a break?"

"HA! Keep me posted when you're eternity years old, buddy," God said. "But sure, take the weekend and relax. You can head back on Sunday."

On Sunday, the Lord created a gateway back to the worlds. Jesus used it to head back to the tomb he was buried in.

The gateways in the caves existed all over the earth; however they only allowed spiritual beings to use them as the doors they are. If a living creature went into the caves, they would be just those...dark and rocky caverns that led into the depths of the earth. They're just big, scary holes to us simple human folk, but the caves are a complex and diverse system of transit. There are pathways to many places: Heaven and Hell, Limbo and Purgatory, Hades and Valhalla, Kansas and Arkansas.

To travel to the land of the dead, any cave would work, but without a map it's a gamble on where you could end up. There is only one map on Earth: A homeless guy named Catfish Durham.

TWENTY-TWO

The group walked in silence down the dark trail on Lookout Mountain. There were no words for how they felt. Catfish led them, with Olivia in the rear, crying. Her phone rang. She bawled harder as she saw who was calling. It was her boyfriend. She didn't answer.

"There is a grotto a few miles away," Catfish said, breaking the quiet. "We can enter the pathways back from there. You two need to get back to Limbo before it's too late."

"The pathways through the caves are impossible to just wander through," BJ replied "How are we supposed to just mosey on back to Limbo? It's a damned maze!"

"I need something to draw on," Catfish said.

* * * * *

The walls of the Hellish caverns echoed with the steps of demons as they marched down the rocky corridors. The Rocky Mountain Division was close, Amauros could feel it. The demonic army was filled with demons of all sorts of different demographics. There were young and old, some very old. It was tough to tell many of them apart, as their time in Hell had greatly disfigured them.

The smell of sulfur was long gone as they had progressed on their journey. It began to smell of minerals from the running water nearby. The air was crisp and musty. Many creatures of the underworld lose some of their worldly senses over time. Such is death. Those that still had their sense of smell had different thoughts come to mind as they grew closer to Limbo, closer to a world with love.

One demon was remembering his childhood. He thought back to being a young boy and finding his father in their basement, fixing a leaky pipe. He had decided to keep his father company and conveniently try out a new pair of roller skates that he had received for Christmas. The unfinished concrete floor was a perfect venue for such a task, all the while breathing in the same stale odor that he was breathing in now, in the caves of the afterlife. To many it was off-putting; to him it smelled like a better time.

The army approached a turn as Amauros ordered them to come to a halt. The demons stood still and looked in amazement as they saw each other and recognized the sheer number of their force. There had never been an attack this size that any of them could think of.

A general approached Amauros.

"Why have we stopped?" he asked the blind Duke of Hell. He had a very whiny voice, with a subtle English accent.

"Just around this corner is the opening to our destination. The sun will be shining through and we will be in sight of the angels. We can't begin our attack until we know that my man on the inside is ready," Amauros answered. "Bring me two soldiers that would be best suited for stealth."

The general disappeared into the crowd of demons behind them. The demons began to sit down and scurry around like rats. They were used to being bored in a dark cave. Amauros began to walk forward alone and approached the turn into the sunlight. Although he could not see, he could feel the light gently warm his pale face. *This is my destiny.*

Destiny is a heavy word. It's hard to give a single moment in time to the thought of destiny. We walk through this earth searching for a meaning and many of us find very little of it. We are slaves to the thought of fate and hopeful in thinking that we pave our own path, but when the chips are down and times are tough we look toward a golden future called *destiny*. A man meets a woman: destiny. A woman has a child: destiny. A man slips on the ice and breaks his neck: destiny. Amauros was no exception. He felt that all of his life and then in his death had led to one thing. He would be the one to take control over Heaven and finally have a place of worth in the only perfect place ever created. He was practically drooling as he felt the sun warm his face.

The general interrupted his moment in the sun. He was with two smaller demons. They were both women from the same town in southern Louisiana. They had both died in a fire back in the early 1900's.

"Sir, these two are…" the general began.

"Ladies…" Amauros interrupted, without turning around, "I need you to find a way to this building and report back to me the status of my man inside. You must do whatever it takes to be secretive. We absolutely cannot be discovered."

The two demons accepted their orders and

disappeared into the sunlight.

"Sir, I don't mean to cause any trouble, but when you interrupt me it makes me look weak in front of those that I oversee. I must keep a level of fear and respect from my soldiers," He said; with the same whiny voice that Amauros despised.

Amauros turned and locked his blackened eyes onto the general's face.

"General, are you familiar with these caves and all of the many worlds that are connected?"

The general stood still and responded, "I've heard about the caves, yes."

"But have you heard of the many places? There are literally thousands of realms all connected by a single system of transportation: these caves. You live in Hell, which is one of the worst places to be. However, have you heard of Bransyn-Myseri?

"No."

"Well, Bransyn-Myseri is another place of punishment and torture; however it's much different than Hell. It was created in the outskirts of the afterlife of another world in another realm. You wouldn't be able to comprehend the contrasts between that place and here. You see, in Hell we still have time. We still have a 'yesterday' and we still have a 'tomorrow' so it gives us a sense of progress. Even though Hell may be torture incarnate, we still have a sense of a future. In one way, this makes it all the more torturous than just suffering because we always know that there is more to come. Bransyn-Myseri, on the other hand, doesn't confine itself to the thoughts of time. The only torture yet to come is already happening but hasn't come yet. Your mind warps and starts working against you. You'll find yourself in darkness alone, with no sense of who you are or where you are going, because you aren't going anywhere, but you're nowhere yet. You find yourself deaf, dumb, and blind alone in a void just knowing that this will last for eternity, but time doesn't move."

The general began, "Sir, I meant no disrespect in my…"

"Shh…" Amauros interrupted again before grabbing him by the throat and lifting him into the air. The nearby demons stopped what they were doing and watched quietly.

"Another question for you, General," he said, as he began carrying him toward ledge, above the running water. "Do you think I became the three hundredth and twenty fourth Duke of Hell by answering to tiny little kittens like you?!"

He held the general out over the abyss. The general tried to say something but couldn't.

Amauros smiled, "Below you is the river, Styx. I'm not sure where it leads from here. For your sake, I hope not Bransyn-Myseri, but I'm really not sure," Amauros hissed.

The general's legs were dangling over the edge. He had a fear in his eyes that he hadn't had since he had first gone to Hell.

"I don't like feedback, General."

With that, Amauros dropped the demon into the river below, sealing his fate into another world and another time. The screams of the general echoed as he disappeared into the violent waters below. The army of demons stood quiet. Maybe their trip into the sunlight wouldn't be as pleasant as they all thought.

TWENTY-THREE

"You know what sounds good?" Catfish said.

He was riding shotgun in Olivia's car as she drove. They were heading down the mountain toward the cave site that Catfish had mentioned.

"What's that, my good man?" BJ asked from the back. He can Colin were crammed in the tiny backseat of her car.

"Some of Mick E. Mouse' famous Garbage Can Margaritas!" The homeless man responded cheerfully.

"I could use a margarita right now," Olivia said.

"Well, after we drop these two off, I know a guy," Catfish said to Olivia.

"Speaking of dropping us off..," Colin started. "Are you absolutely positive that this is the way back?"

Colin had been studying the makeshift map that Catfish Durham had drawn up for them. He had found an old paper bag from the wreckage of Jack's van and used a black sharpie to detail it. It seemed pretty easy to navigate, minus the occasional treacherous stairways and narrow bridges over the unknown.

"What's this strange passage at the bottom?" BJ asked.

"What passage?" Catfish turned around and snagged the map from the Watchers.

"Oh...," he began, "yeah, don't worry about that. That's some kind of stain or something. I tried to smell it and figure out the chemical makeup of it. I think it's one of two things: coffee or urine."

He put his face to it and gave it a big inhale.

"Well, now I'm smelling lemon..,"

*   *   *   *   *

Leah felt hopeless as she tried to rest her eyes. It'd been two days since she was chained against the walls in the boiler room. She knew that if she didn't act soon, nothing would happen.

Leah had died many years ago. She grew up in a medium sized city on the Mississippi River in southern Illinois. Her parents split when she was young, which, like many children of broken homes in that time, gave her both unusual strengths and weaknesses. She was stubborn to a benefit and loyal to a fault, which really only mattered when it came to relationships. There's a certain romance to a woman with those attributes. She'll love a man when he's blindly wrong; yet never admit that he was ever right. It's a sexy balance, but one that wears over time.

It was her senior year of high school, 1979, and she decided that she wanted to be a star. She began planning her trip to Chicago when Evan arrived. She was crazy about him. They had plans to move together, she would be a singer, and he would work in finance. They would take the world by storm.

Evan was in his third year of college, was devilishly

charming, and came from a very affluent family in town.

Rich families in small towns are a breed of their own. So, when Leah told Evan that they were going to be a family of three by the end of the year, it didn't surprise many when he bailed and left Leah to raise a child on her own. It did, however, surprise her. She would have never bailed on someone, especially when they needed her most.

Leah gave birth to a beautiful baby boy just three days before Christmas. She was nineteen years old and alone in the hospital. Her tears of joy were mixed with fear. She took a job at the grocery store downtown and worked as many hours as she could. It was unfair, and she was paid much less than her male coworkers, but still she pushed on. Evan came from money, but he paid very little to help out.

Director Hauser looked up. "Leah are you okay?"

"All things considered...sure."

"Have any bright ideas?"

Leah yelled over to one of the demons, "Hey! Come over here and unchain me so I can beat your ass!"

The demons laughed.

"I'm out of ideas," Leah said.

*   *   *   *   *

The gravel was grinding beneath the tires of Olivia's car as she turned off of the highway. They had a mile to go down this road, then a short hike to the entrance of the cave that Catfish knew.

"So, it shouldn't take longer than an hour or so to get back?" BJ asked.

"No it's not a long walk." Catfish replied.

"So, we get back. We figure out a way to contact the angels, and we get Limbo back in action!" BJ clapped his hands together as he pumped himself up.

Colin didn't share the same enthusiasm. He couldn't let the fact that Jack had gone to Hell be put away. It wasn't guilt that was weighing on him, it was something different. He couldn't help but feel that the system was rigged. It wasn't fair. A man should be able to make his own decisions, not be swayed by outside forces.

"Do you ever question all of this?" Colin asked the jazz man.

"What do you mean?" BJ asked back.

"I mean, I understand we all need to be accountable for our choices, but what about being accountable for the choices that we were pushed or pulled into? How is it that our punishment is solely ours, when the choices we made were not?"

"Well, cat, there's a bigger picture than all of this. It's like we get a second chance to prove where we stand on the balance of good and evil by being Watchers. We get to help others."

"Yeah, but should we have ever even been in Limbo in the first place? I mean, without you pushing me into better decisions, maybe I would have been more of a dickhead and belong in Hell. I don't know."

BJ was quiet.

"Look at Jack, for example," Colin continued. "The guy drank and smoke and tripped and cussed like it was his day job, but he had a good, kind heart. He was an artist and a brother, and he sure as shit didn't deserve to be dragged into all of this crap. If there were no outside forces trying to manipulate him into good or bad choices, I would bet my soul on him choosing to do right on his own."

The car slowed down as they approached the end of the road.

"You may be right, my friend, but it's too late now," BJ said. "Jack's dead and we all know where he is. There was nothing any of us could do."

"Maybe..." Colin responded as he opened the car door and stepped into the dark forest. The entrance to the cave stood out from the trees around them.

"Catfish," Colin questioned, "do you know the way to any other places in these caves?"

"I don't. I was just given the one route. Why? Where else do you want to go?" the homeless prophet responded, even though he already knew the answer.

"BJ is probably right. This is all beyond me. Who am I to question the ways of the universe? I'm just a dead farmer that never did much with my life...or death. I drink wine and watch over a guy that lives his life louder and bolder than I could have ever dreamed. I've been a coward. I've been afraid. I've spent more time thinking 'what if' than ever feeling accomplished. I can say this, though. If the tables were turned and Jack were here and any one of us were there, he wouldn't hesitate to do something about it."

"What are you saying, cat?" BJ asked.

"I'm saying..," Colin took a breath and looked at the caves, "that I'm going into those caves, but I'm not going back to Limbo yet. I'm going to find the way to Hell and I'm going to bring back my friend. I'm breaking Jack out of Hell."

TWENTY-FOUR

The mouth of the cave jutted out of the earth in a jagged way. It reminded Colin of a yawning dog. There was an innocence to the serenity of it, but the jagged teeth-like rocks along the outside of the opening demanded respect. The group was miles away from the nearest town, in the middle of the woods, in the middle of the night. They had just lost a dear friend and had narrowly escaped a couple of demon attacks. While a foreboding cave in the middle of a dark forest might have given most the willies, given the circumstances, this group barely noticed.

It began to lightly snow. The weather in Colorado was a fickle lady. She could scorch your lawn and chill your bones in the same day.

All four of them stepped out of the car together.

"I don't even know what to say," Olivia said.

"You don't have to say anything," Colin responded. "I owe you an apology. I know it was a tough situation between you and Jack. I'm sorry for judging you. Jack really loved you, and I know that you had love for him, although you guys showed it in the weirdest ways."

Olivia was quiet. She did love Jack, despite his frustrating ways. He was a bold spirit and a wild animal. He could bask in the sunshine, but howl at the moon. Olivia needed someone that she could tame. She thought that maybe sometimes who you love isn't the same as who you need. Jack felt differently. He felt that who you love is exactly who you need, despite their flaws. You can't love a person for their potential. He needed Olivia like he needed air, but he was too stubborn to admit it, and often times too drunk to remember it, too.

"Bring him back," Olivia told Colin before hugging him goodbye.

She hugged BJ, thanked the homeless man, sat back into the driver's seat of her car, and drove away. Catfish walked with the two Watchers toward the caves.

"You sure about this?" BJ asked Colin.

"No," Colin laughed nervously, "but it's what I need to do."

"I only know the way to Limbo so I can't help you with a map to Hell, but I can tell you that the further into darkness you get, the closer you are. Don't follow the water," Catfish said.

"Okay, easy enough I guess." Colin looked over at BJ. "Jack and I will catch up with you as soon as we can, but don't wait for us. You have to get back and warn the angels before it's too late."

"I'll handle it, cat. You be careful. We don't need two souls stuck in the pit, and I don't want to have to come after you!"

They looked over at Catfish, but he was already leaving. He turned back before entering the woods and waved. The Watchers returned a wave and walked into the cave together.

They immediately felt the world changing around

them as they stepped toward the dark. There was a gentle glow in the rocks above them. The air felt stale. They knew that they were transitioning between the land of the living and the dead.

Sounds of a babbling creek began to poke through the quiet glow of the cavern. They felt as if they were walking up a moderate slope. They continued closer to the stream. BJ held the dirty map that Catfish had drawn closer toward him. It was difficult to read in the dimly lit cave.

"The map says I need to follow this stream under those rocks." He pointed down the rushing water to a hole in the wall.

The only other place to go was across the narrow water, deeper into the darkness before them.

"Okay. I guess this is where we split then," Colin said.

"No changing your mind on this?"

"I have to do this."

"Stay smooth, cat." BJ hugged him.

Colin jumped over the stream and peered into the distant dark. He turned back to watch the jazz musician check the temperature of the water with his hand. BJ smiled as he dipped into the running water and ducked under the rocky overhang, into the hole.

Colin was alone and he felt it. He knew going into this journey he was going to be facing it by himself, but knowing something and feeling it are not usually the same. He was afraid, and he was sad, and he was alone; and he was heading to Hell.

TWENTY-FIVE

Walking toward Hell is pretty much like one would imagine: warm. Colin could feel the heat on his cheeks as he followed further down the corridor. He rounded a corner, and a room opened up. The glow from a river of lava ahead illuminated the rocks around him. The path led down a narrow trail and onto the cave floor. There was a small rocky bridge that went over the river of lava. Colin couldn't see anywhere else to go but over the bridge.

It was quiet as he walked except for the occasional screams that echoed in the distance. He didn't know much about Hell except from stories he'd heard both back in life and in Limbo. He did know that it was enormous and had many different levels. There was no telling where Jack had gone, though. Unless of course there was a level dedicated to lost rock and rollers. *That actually probably exists.*

He crossed the bridge and continued through the glowing cavern. *I hope BJ is doing okay.*

There was a lot riding on them. None of this was on the job description from his orientation. Colin had never dealt well with pressure. He didn't like to be counted on. He was afraid to fail his entire life. However, with the death of his friend, and the pressure of the fate of the afterworld on his shoulders, he felt strong. It was confidence that he had never possessed before. He knew what he needed to do and walked closer to the scariest and most evil location known to man with conviction. He was ready to dig in and fight.

The glow from the burning river faded as he made his way deeper into the rocks. There was an easy light. However, he couldn't find the source. He could just see the darkness. The heat disappeared. There was no cold, nor movement in the air. There was no sense of temperature at all, just a blank sense on the skin. Colin was numb to air here.

The screams in the distance were cancelled out by the nearby moans of boredom. The Watcher had yet to meet a soul, but was sure he was close to something that used to be alive.

The rocky pathway led to an old wooden door. There were no markings on it. There was nothing in the way of explanation. Colin did what any sensible person who was looking for the entrance to Hell would do and opened it before the fear that flowed through him could stop him.

As he stepped through he saw an open yellow sky. It looked as if it were twilight, with sweeps of pink and orange. It was beautiful. He continued down his rocky pathway until it turned into damp grass. That's when he heard the frantic yelling of someone nearby.

"HELP!"

Colin looked around and scanned the sleepy world around him. He noticed the black silhouettes of mangled trees in the surrounding distances.

Colin stood quietly, hoping to hear something that

might lead him toward the mysterious shout.

"HURRY! BEFORE HE SEES YOU!"

Colin looked to his left and saw a figure hanging from the branches of what appeared to be an old willow tree.

Before who sees me? He began toward the figure. The sounds of wings flapping came from the sky. Colin looked toward it and saw a gigantic creature circling far above. He began to sprint toward the trees and take cover.

"Over here!" the voice hushed to Colin as he neared.

Colin approached the sound and saw a man in a noose, dangling from the tree limbs. He was wearing overalls with a ragged white shirt underneath. His bare feet were exposed and were distorted. He hadn't fully taken on the demon form, but it had begun.

"Where am I?!" Colin whispered in a frenzy.

"Does it look like I've been out exploring?!"

"Is this Hell?"

"I think so. Sort of. Can you get me down?!"

"How did you get here? I'm looking for my friend," Colin asked

"How did I get here?! I fucking died, man. Get me down, please!"

"What is that thing in the sky?!" Colin asked again, ignoring the man's pleas.

"That's Hank, the Demon Camel of Capite."

Hell was comprised of two worlds. Capite and Calcem: The Head and the Heel. Capite was a place of endless waiting. They were the miscellaneous sinners of the world and the suicidal. They were the lucky unfortunate. They suffered both in life and after. It wasn't a place of burning and gnashing, but of waiting and wandering.

Colin was in the outskirts of Capite.

"A camel? I wouldn't have guessed that."

"Have you ever seen a camel, man!? They're terrifying!"

Colin thought about it. *Odd? Yes. Dirty? Probably. Terrifying?* He wasn't sure.

The dangling near-demon spoke again.

"Hey. If you get me down, I'll show you the way to where you want to go."

Colin had no way of cutting the rope. He began to climb the tree. The rope was attached to a limb that was about twenty feet above. He had no problem climbing trees. He grabbed a limb and began to ascend. There was a gravelly scream in the distance. The sounds of Hank, the Demon Camel heralding doom upon his realm.

Colin reached the top and began to shake the limb. He couldn't untie the knot for the time it has been there seemed to almost fuse the rope together. He climbed higher and stood on the limb. I'll have to break it from the tree. He grabbed another limb above his head and held on before he began stomping on the one that the noose was attached. Soon he felt it begin to weaken.

The limb snapped and the man fell to the ground into a heap of old rope and denim. Colin climbed down and helped the man to his gnarled feet.

"What's your name?" Colin asked as the man pulled the noose from off of his neck.

"Wade," he responded. "I've been here for years. Thank you. That was SO boring."

"Okay, Wade..," Colin began, "I'm looking for my friend. He was killed yesterday and doesn't belong here. I'm going to get him out. Where do we go from here?"

"I have to be honest, here. I don't actually know. I hanged myself in Arkansas back in '04, and I've been hanging from this tree ever since."

"You lied to me?"

"This is Hell, man. I'm not the Pope."

* * * * *

When Wade was twenty one, he inherited a small boat repair shop from his father after his death. He was an organized business man and ran it well. Over the years he had expanded it into a few shops throughout Arkansas and was making a very good living. He married the love of his life when he was twenty-eight. He had a dog and a garden. Life was good.

One day his wife came to him and said she was pregnant. Wade was thrilled. He wanted nothing more than to be a father. He spent his free time painting the walls and preparing the nursery. He read books about being fatherhood. He gave his employees a raise.

He was contacted, one day, by a friend of an old friend with an investment opportunity. This friend heard that he was about to have a baby and wanted to help him set up an estate with a simple large investment with a very high rate of return.

Wade invested two hundred thousand dollars and his business as collateral. He began seeing a return the next few months of twenty-three thousand a month. It was looking great. Then the returns stopped. Wade spent weeks trying to contact the friend, but had no luck. It was winter time and there wasn't much business coming in. He had been robbed and was heading toward bankruptcy.

His wife went into labor, and Wade was by her side every step of the way. The baby was born and Wade couldn't believe his eyes. Wade and his wife were white. The baby was black. He was heartbroken that his wife had been cheating, but was still willing to help with the child. Shortly after, she left him and moved in with the child's biological father. It was almost too much to bear.

Then his dog died.

Wade hanged himself and woke up dangling from a willow tree with nothing but a demonic camel there to welcome him.

*   *   *   *   *

"Let's head through these trees and get the hell out of Hell," Wade said.

Colin replied, "No can do. We have to keep going. I'm not leaving here without my friend."

Colin began walking away.

"Wait, what am I supposed to do now?!" Wade whispered.

He didn't have any other choice but to go along with Colin. The two of them headed deeper into the dead forest of Capite.

TWENTY-SIX

BJ gasped for air as he emerged from the stream. He quickly remembered that he had no use for air and his panicking was moot. Old habits die hard though, and a man doesn't easily forget the fear that comes from the thought of drowning.

His suit was soaked and was dripping as he climbed out of the stream and rolled onto his back. He looked at his surroundings and saw beams of light shining through the cave from holes in the ceiling. As he lay in the puddle, he peered up toward the source and saw a blue sky through the small holes.

He opened the map and tried to make sense of Catfish's drawing. It looked like there were two ways of getting to Limbo. The first one had at least three hundred stairs, the second one had zero stairs. BJ chose the latter. He stood up and began to slush his way further into the caves.

It's a strange thing to at one moment be a part of a team with a shared mission and then to jump into a stream to find yourself completely alone in a dark pathway between worlds. Loneliness has a way of creeping up on you. There was a longing inside of him and he felt the aches of being scared and alone. BJ thought about his mother. When he was scared or sad as a child, she would rock him back to comfort on their old wooden porch. Chrissy would climb up and join them on her other knee. Loneliness hits twins harder than most.

They grew up in the outskirts of a small town in central Illinois. As kids they would spend time in the surrounding woods building forts in the fallen trees and playing with their dog. They helped their mother with laundry and played in the clothes as they hung from the line, waving like flags in the wind.

When they were older their mother saved enough money to buy a radio and the twins began to fall in love with the sounds of New Orleans style jazz. They would listen along to the Fletcher Henderson band and pretend to play along to Louis Armstrong's solos.

One day Chrissy came home with a trumpet and gave it to his brother. When asked how he came about it, Chrissy would say that he had found it in the garbage in one of the alleys in town. BJ knew the truth. He knew that his brother had stolen the instrument, but the thought of the repercussions kept him from saying anything. A young black kid getting caught stealing something from a white shop owner would not bode well, and BJ was anything if not loyal to his brother. They hid the stolen trumpet in the woods near one of their childhood forts.

Over time they would sneak off to the woods and take turns playing it. It came naturally to BJ. He would learn to bend the notes and breathe and eventually figured out the scales. Chrissy struggled to keep up and began sneaking off alone to emulate his brother. Over time he learned the instrument and found himself confident in his abilities.

BJ began taking piano lessons as well and soon abandoned the brass for the strings. He was a quick learner and a creative player. Chrissy always felt a few steps behind.

When they were seventeen they decided to start a band and pursue their passions. The Twins began to book gigs at the local speakeasies and were making money before they knew it. As they began to grow their fan base, their animosity toward each other did the same.

Get up and get moving. BJ sat up and took off his clothes to ring them out. After they were somewhat dry he got dressed and began to walk, following the makeshift map along the way. He was humming to himself and enjoying the reverberation from his voice as it bounced through the caverns.

After what felt like an hour of walking, he stopped in his tracks. He could hear voices in the distance. He crept further and slowly rounded the corner to look out toward an army of demons. Beyond them was a giant opening with a sunlit field outside. He had made it back to Limbo.

Now what do I do? BJ thought to himself. His only way back was blocked by an army of demons. He was trapped.

*   *   *   *   *

Chrissy was staring at his hands. He was naked, sitting in the orientation room, just outside the door to the waiting room. It had been a long time since he had seen his hands in their human form. He felt strange. It was almost like he was stronger, however he was smaller. He no longer resembled the monstrous gorilla like creature he had gotten used to.

A demon walked into the room with some clothes. It was a track suit he had stolen from one of the jailed Watchers.

"Como usted pregunto," the demon said. He handed the clothes to Chrissy.

Chrissy grabbed the track suit and put it on. It was a little small on the lean black man's new form, but it worked.

"Cualquier otra cose que pueda hacer?" the demon asked.

"Huh? Oh uh…yeah it fits okay."

"Busque a otros, pero estos parecia el mas comodo." The demon smiled.

"Oh…um…yeah I'm not sure where the bathroom is, man. There's probably a comodo in the hallway, maybe."

"Es un poco pequena, pero se ve bien."

" Look I'm going to be honest; I have no clue what the hell you are saying," Chrissy responded.

"Que?" The demon asked.

"K, thank you, amigo."

"Te nada, amigo."

"I'm not your amigo?"

"Que?"

"What?"

"No comprendo." the demon shook his head

"You said, 'te not a amigo'. Doesn't 'te' mean 'you?' Isn't amigo a friend? You're not my friend?"

"No….TE NADA, amigo."

"Yeah I heard you before. Screw you, man! I'm not your friend?"

"Que?"

"K?! No, not OK! I was reaching out, man! Why don't you comprendo this: you are an el dickhead-o!"

The demon stood silent and confused.

"Also this track suit is too tight! My nuts are all jumbled together and it isn't a comfortable situation down there! They're supposed to be next to each other, not on top of one another. It looks like two thirds of a snowman down there. There isn't anyone in this entire division that has sweatpants?!"

The demon stood in silence, confused.

"….que?"

"YOU SON OF A BITCHO!" He grabbed the demon by the neck and pulled his other hand back to deliver a punch to the cabeza.

The language barrier was broken by the sounds of the orientation room door opening. Two lady demons walked into the room.

"Amauros sent us to check on your progress. Are we ready to begin?" One of the lady demons spoke up.

Chrissy took a deep breath and got himself together. He let go of the Spanish demon's neck and straightened out his skin tight track suit.

"Tell Amauros that everything here is ready. The Watchers are all trapped in their rooms. I have some prisoners in the boiler room. I'm back in my human form and waiting by the waiting room, ready to take my brother's place. Also, this asshole here is NOT my friend." Chrissy nodded his head toward the Spanish speaking demon and then continued. "Tell him I'm ready. Let's begin the first attack."

TWENTY-SEVEN

Colin and Wade were walking quietly through the mangled forest, keeping an ever present eye on the sky for the evil camel that guards it. Colin's eyes had gotten used to the twilight, while Wade's feet were still catching up to the feeling of grass. While the grass of Capite was obviously more evil than the grass of Heaven, it isn't that noticeable.

"Any idea of where your friend is?" Wade whispered to Colin.

"No clue. I've never been here before. I don't even know where to begin looking."

"I've met a few people while I was hanging in that tree over the years. Every now and then someone is trying to escape their punishment and they find their way to Capite. Some of them have gotten close..," Wade continued. "Hank is always watching. Anyway, I've heard some stories of places. It seems that they have a place for everyone."

"What have you heard?" Colin asked.

"Just brief stories really. One lady told me about where she was kept. It didn't have a name, it was just a big room filled with freezing water. She had been floating there for a really long time. Said she escaped when the guards changed shifts. She's probably back there now. It's a shame. She seemed nice."

"Well, she must have done something to be there. Jack is innocent though. He doesn't deserve to be here."

"Everyone has made mistakes, man."

Colin remained silent. His new companion was right. However, some mistakes are worse than others.

"Usually what I hear, though, is that the punishment fits the crime. Rapists get raped. Violent people get beaten. Liars and cheats and con artists are all put in the same room and forced to do Cross Fit. What did your friend do?"

"That's a great question..," Colin answered.

He thought about it for a little bit. Jack had partied a lot. He was an ornery kid, but had a great family life. He wasn't violent, nor a liar. He was just a free spirit in a locked up world.

They came to the edge of the forest and saw a huge wooden bridge over an enormous pit. It appeared to be the only way out. At the end of the bridge was a doorway in the cliff walls.

"How are we gonna cross this without Hank seeing us?! If he sees us we're doomed…more."

Colin looked to the sky. It was clear.

"Only thing to do is run. Let's go."

Without thinking twice Colin was off and running. Wade sighed, and took off as well. They ran as fast as they could down the hill to the bridge and over it. A terrible scream was heard in the distance behind them. Hank had seen them, but for some reason did not pursue them. I guess there was no point if they were already heading deeper into Hell on their own.

They reached the door. It was made of iron and looked heavy and ancient, with claw marks and rust. It screeched as it slowly opened and behind it was a long hallway with old, dirty carpet. Torches lined the walls and lit up the corridor. Water dripped from the high ceilings forming small pools of water throughout.

They no longer felt alone. There were moans and groans of agony and boredom in the distance. A lazy haze of smoke floated above them. It was hot and humid and Colin knew that they were heading in the right direction. Without speaking, they slowly walked forward through the halls of Hell.

*   *   *   *   *

BJ was waiting in the darkness. He had positioned himself behind a set of boulders that were about ten feet away from the entrance he had found himself. The demons beyond him were wandering around, every now and then one would peak its head out of the cave's mouth trying to get a peak of the sunlight before getting whipped and reprimanded by what appeared to be a superior. He knew that his brother must be around somewhere, but he wasn't sure exactly where.

The two smaller creatures had returned to the cave and were talking with a hooded figure who seemed to be in charge. After a few minutes of talking together, the hooded figure walked gracefully toward the army and began directing them to get organized. They all lined up, and before BJ could figure out what his move would be, a small portion of the army marched out of the cave and toward the division.

I'm too late! BJ panicked and started to jump out from his hiding spot. He thought that maybe he could somehow out run them and beat them to the division. Before he could begin his last ditch effort, he saw that a huge majority of the army stayed behind. They were waiting for something.

He sat there scrambling for a plan. He could attempt to sneak past the largest army of demons he had ever witnessed in his afterlife. He could keep hiding behind those boulders. He could head back the other direction in an effort to somehow find another way around. He could fight. None of these options sounded like winners to him.

He peaked back out toward the mouth of the cave. He had been in the darkness of the caves for so long that the greens in the grass almost lit up in the sunlit field. His heart was heavy with helplessness. He decided that maybe he should just walk away and let things be. He was outnumbered and out of ideas. Then he saw a small figure walking in the field. Some of the demons saw it too, and a small commotion began as they all looked toward it.

A light colored dog was walking toward them through the field. Its hair was curly and blond. As it neared the middle of the field, it sat down and stared at them from the distance. At that moment the cave began to rumble. The demons all tried to hold their balance as the ground gently shook. All of a sudden a large piece of rock fell loose from the upper walls of the cave, exposing the sky. The boulder fell to the ground and landed strongly in the center of the army, crushing any unlucky creature that didn't get out of the way in time.

As the demons got back into line and the rumbling stopped, they looked outside to see that the dog had vanished.

The commotion quieted, and the demons lined back

up and resumed their Hellish waiting game. BJ began to panic again until he noticed something. The light that shone through the newly formed hole in the wall illuminated the cave walls near him. There were jagged rocks and grooves and BJ had another idea. He could climb up and over and escape through the hole. He had never rock climbed before, but in his position he didn't seem to have any other choice. *Not like I could die from the fall. What's the worst thing that could happen? I suppose I could fall from the ceiling and land in the middle of an enormous demonic army that's waiting to take over Limbo.* BJ sighed and wiped his palms on his pant legs.

He snuck toward the wall and began to climb.

TWENTY-EIGHT

The two had been walking for what seemed like hours and had gotten nowhere. The hallway remained the same and as they walked further down it, they only felt further away from their destination. It was maddening.

"An endless hallway on the path to Hell; you'd have thought they would have been a little more creative," Colin said in a frustrated tone.

"It beats hanging in a tree," Wade replied.

"Well, while we're spinning our tires here, Jack is somewhere suffering and Limbo is being held hostage. We need to figure something out soon. I hope BJ made it in time."

"Who's BJ?" Wade asked.

"He's my Watch……friend. He's my friend."

"What's the 'BJ' stand for? Brad Johnson? Brent Jackson? Barthalamue Jeoffrey Smithers?"

"I don't know actually…I just always went with BJ."

"You don't know your friend's name?"

Colin felt kind of ashamed. He had plenty of opportunities to learn more about his Watcher, but he was too focused on himself and his own worries.

"Let's turn around; maybe we missed something behind us?" a frustrated Colin said.

There were no better ideas to be had. The two of them turned back. The humidity was exhausting. It was the first time Colin had felt this tired in a very long time. They walked for only fifteen minutes and found themselves staring at a dead end.

"There was a door here, right?" Wade demanded. He started to feel the wall as though maybe there was something he was missing.

"Yes," Colin answered quietly. They were stuck in an endless hallway. Welcome to Hell.

* * * * *

It was 1963. Colin awoke to his mother shaking him. "Wake up, darling."

It was summer time, and a ten year old Colin was enjoying his time off from school. He didn't fit in well with the students at his elementary school. It was a private Catholic school with a hefty tuition. Colin's mother taught there which allowed him to attend the school for free. This was good for Colin because he did not come from money unlike most of his classmates, and his classmates didn't often let him forget it.

Colin helped his father out with chores around the farm. He would feed and water the animals, clean the pens, and do his best with helping his father with general maintenance. The summer months were no break and he would often be given more responsibilities.

"I'm up," Colin would groggily fib to his mother.

"Your father needs you out back on the deck."

Colin dragged his feet out of bed and slowly got dressed. The sun was up, and his father had already been working on rebuilding one of the fences. Colin tied his shoes and walked out back to join his dad.

The dry Colorado heat was disguised by a cool, gentle breeze. There wasn't a cloud in the sky, and the land around put the horizon further away than normal.

"Good morning, Son," his father said.

"How's the fence?" Colin asked, pretending to be eager to help out.

"Oh, the fence is coming along just fine, but I have a special project for you. There's a hornet's nest underneath the deck here. We need to go under and get it out of there. These damned hornets are taking over our deck."

He handed Colin a bucket with a bottle of Raid in it, some gloves, and a handkerchief to cover his face with.

"I have to go under the deck?" Colin asked, now wide awake and a little nervous.

"Well, I'm afraid I can't fit under there. I'm too big. This is a job for a big man in a little body." His father smiled at him.

They walked around to the side of the deck where his father had already removed one of the side walls of the deck. Colin could already see a couple hornets flying around. The opening was probably four feet wide by four feet tall.

Colin grabbed the bucket and reluctantly entered the opening. He couldn't let his father see the fear in his face, so he quickly covered it with the bandana and moved forward. It was cold dirt underneath, and the only light was the light shining through the cracks between the deck boards above him. He could hear the hornets buzzing and began to search for the nest. He finally spotted it in the furthest spot possible. It was deep in the corner where the deck met the foundation of the house.

"Find it?" his father yelled underneath.

"It's in the corner," Colin whispered back, afraid that the hornets would hear him.

He slowly moved through the dirt and slalomed his way around the few short support beams holding the deck floor up. As he inched closer to the nest, he could feel the hornets flying around him. He was desperate to keep calm and noticed a large hole underneath the foundation of the house. It looked like it went deeper under the house. Colin made a mental note to tell his father about it when he got out.

The nest was a few feet away from him now. He positioned himself against the concrete foundation and slowly pushed the bucket underneath the nest.

He grabbed the Raid in one hand and the wooden rod in the other and slowly held them up toward the nest. A hornet landed on his outstretched arm and he froze, waiting. As soon as it flew away, Colin closed his eyes and sprayed the can onto the nest. He immediately began scraping it from its base, and the nest dropped into the bucket. Colin scrambled to shove the lid on it and sealed the nest. He sighed in relief. Then he felt the stings.

It was like electricity with each one. Pain shot through his arm and then his neck and ear. He panicked and began swatting the air as he fell over desperate to escape. There was no time to think through the pain, and he threw himself into the hole he had found minutes before.

The cool mud was a welcome change in sensation. The stings stopped, and he lay still for a moment. His father heard the commotion and was yelling at his son from outside the deck.

"You okay?!"

Colin didn't answer yet. He was spinning from the moment.

"COLIN! ARE YOU OKAY IN THERE?!"

"Uh..I think so. Yeah. Yeah I got stung a bunch and I'm in a hole under the house. I think they all flew off. I got the nest."

"You got the nest in the bucket?"

"Yeah."

"Good work. What are you waiting for? Get out of there!"

"Well…I think I'm stuck."

Colin's foot was stuck between the mud and the underside of the hole in the foundation. It seemed as if he was in the remnants of an old crawlspace. He felt his heart speed up and began to panic. He was trapped between mud and concrete and scared to death. The way out of the hole was a few feet away from him, but it felt like a much larger distance. The bandana was hot over his face so he took it off and breathed in the musty smell of the wet dirt.

"How are you stuck?"

"My foot is stuck in the mud and pinned to some concrete."

"How'd you get it in there?"

"I don't know. I'm scared!" Colin began to tear up.

His father got down and pulled through the dirt toward the top of the hole.

"Colin," he said gently, "close your eyes, take a deep breath, and look toward me."

Colin regained control over his tears and listened to his father. He opened his eyes and looked toward the opening. He couldn't see his dad, but he knew he was there.

"Okay..," Colin said.

"Sometimes all you can do is push through the fear, kid."

Colin looked down at his foot and began to rotate it. After a moment it came loose, and he crawled toward the hole and out of the deck.

*   *   *   *   *

Wade sat down against the wall that used to be a door. He was confused and lost and felt that maybe he just made a bad situation worse for himself.

"I should have just kept my mouth shut. Hanging in that tree wasn't so bad. At least I had a nice skyline to look at!" He said despairingly.

Colin looked around. There was nothing to look at but a deep damp hallway leading to who knows where or how long it will take to get there. He, too, was losing his grip and felt that maybe he made the wrong choice. He is no match for the greater powers in the Heavens and Hells. He was just a boring farmer with no initiative to be great, let alone some sort of hero of the afterlife. He just wanted some wine and to sit in the couch in his Watcher's quarters and listen to Jack write a song with his band. That was the highlight of his death. Jack could write a hell of a song.

He sat down next to his new friend.

"So you killed yourself, huh?" Colin asked.

"How'd you guess?" Wade responded.

"Well the noose was kind of a hint."

They both mustered up some laughter.

"I killed myself in the heat of the moment. I regret it, but there's no going back now. I ams what I ams and I dids what I dids."

"I thought about it before," Colin said. He wasn't sure why he was opening up to Wade. Maybe it was their newfound predicament of being nowhere for possible a very long time.

"Yeah?" Wade asked.

"Yeah. I think everyone does sometimes. They may not ever give it a serious thought, but I think everyone wonders about it. Some of us are built for it, others aren't. I don't know. I'm no expert. Whenever I thought about it, I thought mostly about how others would react. I wanted to feel important, but I never knew how. I guess I thought maybe offing myself would have been a way to have the spotlight. I never wanted to do it though."

"I guess I thought about it that way too, before. Back when I first got married, all I wanted was for my wife to be nice to me. I didn't need dinner on the table or a martini ready when I walked in. I just wanted her to be nice. I sometimes thought, if I were dead maybe she would realize what she took for granted. When I actually did it, though, it wasn't for any spotlight or validation. I just didn't see any way out. Kind of like our situation now. Dead end, ya know?"

"Was it scary?" Colin asked

"No...it was kind of peaceful. But it was a mistake," Wade said quietly.

Colin stared ahead. "An 'every breath's a gift' kinda thing?"

"It's all about attitude, man."

Colin felt a sting on his left arm. He immediately winced and slapped the source of it, dropping whatever it was to the ground. Colin looked down and next to his foot he saw a dead hornet.

"It's a hornet..," Colin said confusedly.

"Well, that's odd."

"No, it's not..." Colin stood up and began walking down the hallway. It was a message.

"I take it we're not looking for the door?" Wade asked.

"We push through the fear."

Wade jumped to his feet and they continued down the hallway into the unknown.

They walked along the halls of Hell, their steps making squishy noises in the wet carpet. Something felt different to Colin. He knew that they would see something soon. He was imagining what all existed in a place like this. It was very unpleasant, but there wasn't yet the burning and toasting and gnashing of teeth like he had been told as a kid. Mostly it was just boredom.

As they walked, they noticed that the walls began to slowly change colors. It went from a dull and dirty yellow to a deep orange. The smoke began to thicken above them. Soon, they could hear the groans and moans again. They were getting closer.

Up ahead, Colin could see something glowing. It was circular and reflecting a dull white light. As the two of them neared the source, they found the end of the hallway. It was an opening with an abrupt drop off into an enormous rocky pit lit up by the red glows of fiery embers embedded into the rocks. They looked toward the glowing circular object that they had seen in the distance. It was a gigantic clock that was showing six o'clock.

The souls below were walking around barely acknowledging each other. Up ahead was a huge drop off with no way to cross it. A narrow wooden drawbridge stood pointing straight up leaving the wandering souls trapped on the other end.

TWENTY-NINE

Colin and Wade stood high above, in the end of the hallway. They only way to get down was to either scale the flat wall or jump. Colin sat down and dangled his legs over the edge of the wall, and before he could think of something clever to say, he let himself drop.

He could feel the friction on his ass as he slid toward the bottom.

He crumpled as he landed at the bottom. It was a long fall, and he stayed on the ground a moment to shake off the impact. Wade landed next to him.

The two stood up and dusted themselves off. They looked around their surroundings to see a herd of slowly wandering souls, not yet in the shape of demons. There were men and women, young and old, just walking around. Colin began walking through them, asking if they had seen a young man with a bushy beard and scraggly hair.

"His name is Jack..," Colin was asking desperately. He was mostly ignored.

"Shhhhh," some of them would whisper.

"Let's split up?" Wade said.

"Okay..," Colin said. He felt exhausted.

They split away from each other and Wade approached a group of elderly women. Colin kept moving closer toward the drawbridge. A man wearing a leather jacket walked passed him.

"Excuse me, but I'm looking for someone." He stopped the leather clad man. "His name is Jack, and he has a bushy beard and shaggy hair and was wearing a polo shirt with a restaurant logo on it...it was a pepper I think....but odds are he took it off between the last time I saw him and now."

"Shhhhh...," the man put his finger up to his mouth and then pointed to the top of the drawbridge.

Three winged demons sat on top of the bridge like gargoyles. They were keeping watch over the herd of wandering souls. One was holding a pitchfork. The second was holding a whip. The third was holding a taser.

Beyond the bridge was a large wooden door.

Colin looked over at Wade. The elderly ladies had kept walking away, but Wade was holding one of them back. It looked as though he was frustratingly trying to get some sort of response. She began to pull her arm from his grip. Colin looked back at the watching demons. One of them pointed toward the commotion that Wade was causing. Another demon spread his wings as he prepared to fly.

Colin took off in a sprint toward Wade. He grabbed him by the arm.

"Leave her alone man, we're being watched," he said quietly but forcefully.

Wade let go of her and looked at Colin with

confusion. Colin led him behind a nearby boulder.

"Look out above the gates," Colin said.

Wade looked around the boulder.

"Oh....those guys are scary. Is that a taser?!"

They hid behind the boulder for a moment and thought about their move. The demons seemed to relax and continue their vigil. An old man slowly walked passed them and turned his head toward them.

"Hey, you jackasses have been asking about Jack?"

Colin was shocked.

"Yeah..!?" he answered in a hushed voice.

"He was here earlier. Walk with me, but don't make a scene. I don't want to get my balls tasered!"

Colin and Wade hurried over and caught up with the old man. They began to walk at the slow pace the man was meandering.

"So do you know where Jack is?" Colin whispered.

"That young man came in here a day ago it seemed. Don't know. Hard to tell with that danged ol' clock up there that don't work. It's almost like they want us to forget about time. Not like it matters I 'spose. We're gonna be here for now on. Don't matter if it's a minute or a day or an eternity," the old man claimed in a horse voice.

"So what happened?!" Colin asked. They were walking so slowly it was difficult to keep the same pace as the old man.

"This is the first place any of us have been to down here. It's where we wait until they're ready for us. That Jack seemed to be someone important because they had his place ready quicker than Mexican grass goes through a Canadian goose. I felt bad for the kid. Them demons came down here and told him that Ol' Scratch had a special room for him and that anyone that didn't belong down here but still came down here got the special treatment. Then that damned demon tasered that young man right in his testicles. That Jack looked like a bear of a man, but I ain't never heard no bear make them sounds before."

"Jesus Christ..," Colin said.

Everyone groaned in agony.

"Sorry..," Colin whispered to the crowd of people around him. "Then what happened?!"

"Well, then they lowered that bridge and drugged him off over it. I'm not sure where they took him…but if you see him, tell him that Lincoln Duncan says hello and give him his shirt back." He handed Colin a sweaty polo shirt.

"I knew he'd be shirtless..," Colin said.

"It's hot down here, and he said that he had overactive sweat glands. He also told me about Olivia. She sounds like a confused one."

"She's not so bad..," Colin couldn't believe he was defending her, but after the day's events, she deserved a teammate.

"That's what he said."

"So how do we get that bridge down?" Colin asked.

"Hell if I know. They only lower it when it's time to take one of us across it. After they taser our testicles, that is!"

"Whoa, hold up now. I didn't sign up for no testicle tasing," Wade interrupted.

THIRTY

The army was quiet as BJ slowly made his way across the cave walls above them. He was moving horizontally across the dome shaped cavern toward the newly formed hole above the entrance. Rock climbing was never the jazz man's bag, but left without any other choice he had to learn on the go. One wrong move and he would fall right into the midst of the demonic battalion below him. Without Colin, he knew that he was the only hope of warning everyone in Limbo that there was about to be an attack, and he couldn't help but feel it in his gut that he might already be too late.

BJ felt the sunshine of Limbo on his face as he poked his head through the hole. It was a tight fit to squeeze through, but he managed to get out as stealthily as possible. The climb down to the grassy fields was easy. He followed the walls of the caves toward the adjacent tree line in order to stay out view of the army. He could follow the tree line up and go around the building and walk right into the front doors.

*   *   *   *   *

Colin and Wade were hiding behind the hellish boulder. They needed a plan to get through the iron gates of Hell without being seen by the gargoyle-like demons perched high above. Jack was somewhere beyond those doors and Colin was committed to bringing him back.

"Dammit, we're stuck," Colin said in hushed frustration.

Lincoln Duncan was walking back toward them. He had been continuing to wander around so as to not give notice to the guards.

"You boys still trying to get through those gates?"

Lincoln was an old man. He was born poor. He lived poor. He died poor. His father was a fisherman in the Maritimes of eastern Canada. When he was old enough he moved away and headed south for New England in hopes to find some meaning to a restless life.

It was there that he met a girl preaching in a parking lot. She was reading from the Bible and singing hymns. He was infatuated with her and finally felt like maybe his path in life had been revealed. It was enlightening and scary. Later that night he went to her, and they went off to the woods together and Lincoln finally became a man.

Although Lincoln thought this to be his saving grace, it ended up being the beginning of a long life headed toward Hell. When she moved on to another town, he began to booze and gamble and womanize. Sin, like many things, gets easier with practice.

"People don't belong down here, Lincoln," Wade said.

"Some of us do..," Lincoln answered. "I've never really done much for others in my life. I guess I was so busy trying to scratch out a living that I missed the whole point. I've cheated and lied to get ahead. I've stolen things... I still wonder about the many people that I've screwed over. I wonder how much damage my doings have done. Hell, I may have caused some awful things when I think about it. I've earned this."

"You may think you belong here, but Jack doesn't," Colin said.

The old man looked at Colin and nodded in agreement. He would never have had the balls to come down here to rescue his friend. In fact, in Lincoln's long life, he never really had a real friend. Except for her... He would have risked it all for her. She was the only friend he ever really knew. Maybe this was his chance to do something right.

"Okay, boys. I suppose I can help out. Stay behind this rock, and when the time comes you boys run across that bridge and through those gates and go find your friend and take him home."

The old man walked slowly away back into the crowd of wandering souls, all waiting for their turn to enter the gates of Hell. He would cause a distraction for the Watchers. He had finally accepted his fate, and he knew that if there was one more chance to do a good thing he was going to do it, and he knew exactly how to help.

When Lincoln first arrived in Hell, he was scared. He was alone in a sea of estranged souls and didn't understand what was happening. He asked a man for help. His name was Tom. Fucking Tom was an asshole.

"Welcome to Hell you old bitch." Tom said. Then he knocked the old man down and took his shoes. Fucking

Tom.

Lincoln thought back to this as he meandered through the zombie like crowd of the condemned. *Where are you?* He had a score to settle and couldn't think of a better time or reason. As he searched for his nemesis he almost felt like he was alive again. Finally, he reached a small group of people gathered by the wall of the pit. Tom was among them.

Lincoln walked slowly through the group.

"Hey Tom…"

Tom looked up toward the old man and began to laugh. The crowd snickered along with him.

"Can I help you, grandpa?" he said as he crossed his arms in indifference.

Lincoln looked down toward his feet and motioned toward them. "Hope you like the shoes. I forgot to mention…they come with a pair of socks!"

With that, Lincoln Duncan socked the shoe thief right in the jaw and chaos erupted. It was an all out brawl with the old man delivering punch after punch to the downed Tom.

"Holy shit!" Wade whispered in shock. "This place is starting to grow on me."

"The bridge is lowering!" Colin pointed.

A siren was blaring in the distance as the iron gates of Hell were slowly screeching open. The three guards ran out and began to move toward the rioting souls.

The ground shook as the demons landed in the midst of the battle royal, shocking some of the souls into backing away from the fight in fear. Those who were too involved in beating each other suffered the might of the demonic guards as they moved through the crowd. There were back hands and pimp slaps galore, until they reached the dead guy pretzel that was Lincoln and Tom.

Their legs were interlocked as Lincoln tried to put Tom into a choke hold. They didn't notice the demons until two of them broke the fight up and each held the other back. The third demon pulled a taser out of his utility belt and walked toward Tom first. The taser sizzled the air.

"Hey Tom!" Lincoln yelled, with his arms held behind him. "How do you like your nuts?!"

Tom looked at the guard with the fear of God in his eyes.

"I hope you like 'em roasted!" Lincoln laughed maniacally.

The guard zapped Tom in the testicles without mercy. The screams echoed through the cavern and no one noticed as Colin and Wade slipped quietly over the bridge and through the gates, deeper into Hell.

THIRTY-ONE

"Kevin, how hard is it to shit in a box?!"

Meow. Kevin looked up innocently.

"I'm not kidding around! Seriously, it's right here! It's right....get off of me, Darren! God damn you!"

Meow. Darren rubbed against the leg.

"Look at this! There are TWO piles next to the box. It's almost like you're trying to miss!"

Kevin rolled over and stretched his legs.

"I can't take this anymore...and you, Brent...acting like you're some sort of prize, you fucking prima donna. I'd have you neutered if I thought you actually had a pair."

Brent did not react.

"This place is a mess. Where's the broom? There's litter all ov...GOD DAMN IT DARREN! GET OFF OF ME!"

Meowwww. Darren flew through the air.

Jack shook the feline from his leg with anger. It landed

back into a group of wandering cats, all meowing and purring and rolling around in general apathy. There were at least three dozen of them. There were young and old ones. There were shaved ones, mangy ones. All of them were waiting for him.

"WHY IS THERE NO BROOM IN HERE?!"

It had only been a day, but it had felt like years. Time moves strangely in Hell. In an eternal damnation there is no real need for time, so it just carries on with a different weight. You lose track of it quickly. You eventually stop caring about it, but you can still feel it move by.

Jack had been welcomed into Hell much differently than most others. It was known right away who he was and that his punishment would be different, so he was expedited to the front of the line, just barely getting to know one old man named Lincoln before the gates opened for him.

Punishments in Hell were often times pretty creative. Sure you can broil and flay and toil away all of the livelong day, but a true punishment gets to the root of the person. It attacks their essence, and the essence of Jack was nothing if not a big dumb dog with a heart made of gold. And what could be a worse fate for a big dumb loveable mutt like Jack?

*   *   *   *   *

"Cats?" Jack said.

Jack was standing in a red lit courtroom and his sentence was read aloud by a demon in a black judge's robe. Behind him was a crowd of demons watching and snickering.

"Yes, that is what I have decreed. You will be put in a cell full of cats…two dozen!"

"Huh?" Jack said to himself, unsure of what to think.

"What's a matter, Jack? Cat…got your…tongue?!" The judge questioned, holding back his amusement.

The demons in the crowd laughed and laughed at the obvious joke.

"Well, I guess… I guess I'm just confused… I AM in Hell right?" Jack asked suspiciously.

"Yes. Your soul is now ours. Welcome to the darkest darkness found in the deepest depths of the blackest blackness that can only be measured by the most miserable misery of.."

"Yep, yeah, I heard you the first five times…miserable misery and longest length with the smelliest smells blah blah blah…Guys you are basically describing my van at this point…but just so I can clarify… I am in Hell, the most horrible place of torture known to man…and you guys are just going to put me in a room with some cats?"

"TWO DOZEN CATS!" the judge reminded him.

The demons snickered.

"That's it? There's nothing else? I'm going to be in a room with two dozen cats? That doesn't sound so bad."

The judge scoffed.

"Fine, smart ass! THREE DOZEN!" He bellowed with all of the authority of the ancient world.

The demons snickered again. Clearly this fool was only making it worse.

"You guys," Jack said as he looked around the room "it's just some cats. I was expecting to be like…I don't know… beaten with sticks or skinned alive or put upside down in oil or something."

"Trust me; you're going to wish you were put upside down in oil. Our analysts all agreed on this particular punishment. Three dozen cats for eternity?! No one is that strong."

"Wow, okay. Hell, make it four dozen. I was expecting so much worse."

"Well Mr. Cat Lover wants some more cats, does he? FINE! FOUR DOZEN CATS WILL FOREVERMORE BE YOUR DOOM!"

A demon shuffled up and whispered into the judge's ear.

"Really? That's surprising," The judge whispered back before he continued to Jack. "Well, unfortunately we do not actually have four dozen cats available at the moment. But know this, hippie: When we get some more they are heading straight for you. Maybe if you play your cards right, we'll give you a laser pointer for good behavior."

"Sounds great. Can I go meow?" Jack asked, rolling his eyes.

"What did you just say?!"

"I said, 'Can I go now?'"

"Really? Because it sounded like you said 'meow.'"

"What?"

"Instead of 'now.'"

"I'm not following."

"It sounded like you said 'can I go meow.'"

"Nope. Not what I said. You must be hearing things. Are you sure you're feline okay?"

The demons tried to hide their laughter.

"Jack Charlton, you are hereby sentenced to eternity in cell 333. TAKE HIM AWAY!" the judge pounded a gavel made of bones with all the rage that he could muster.

A demonic bailiff grabbed Jack by the arms and began to walk him out of the room.

"Oh oh! Real quick... what's the weed situation down here?" Jack yelled back toward the judge. "Are we all pretty cool, or what?"

The bailiff hit him in the leg with a stick and they took

him away.

* * * * *

The room was musty. Its atmosphere had a red tint to it but no source could be found. There was one large window with light blue sheer blinds. Outside was a beautiful spring day. It was a view of a grassy park with oak trees and the occasional cloud in the light blue sky. Jack imagined that they made it this way just to remind the prisoner that they'll never feel the sunshine again. The door was made of steel, and there were rivets all around the edges that were sharp to the touch.

The floor was covered in thin, damp carpet. It smelled like pet cleaner. There were stains in the corners and the occasional unraveling of the fabric that was most likely caused by those god-damned cats.

A few litter boxes lined one of the walls, as well as a few carpeted play boxes on the opposite. There were a plethora of feather-on-a-sticks and little plastic balls with bells inside, as well as paper bags and balls of yarn strewn across the floor.

Jack walked in and was a little bothered by the fact that the cats didn't even notice. In fact, Jack had to go out of his way to get to meet his new roommates. After a few hours of cleaning up hairballs and wiping litter from his bare feet he knew that the judge was right. This was going to be a nightmare.

One of the cats, an old mangy one that Jack had dubbed Starshine, was sitting at the window and making clicking noises. She was fixated on a bush outside. Jack recognized the chirping noise as something cats would do when they are in a trance like state before attacking a mouse or a bird or some other non threatening bottom rung on the food chain. Jack couldn't help but feeling sad for her.

"I know how you feel, Starshine," he said kindly as he joined her at the window. "It's like we live our whole lives running down our dreams. We work and work and work just to keep our goals in our sights, and yet we still just end up dead and in a room full of cats...or worse I suppose."

Starshine yawned in ambivalent agreement.

"Do you ever feel like you've wasted it? Your life I mean. Sometimes I wonder if I was selfish to focus on music, and not get a real job with a real house and a real yard. Maybe things would have worked out better with Olivia. I could have been a family man. I would have been a good dad."

Starshine jumped down from the window and walked away without looking back

"Oh I'm sorry. Am I boring you?! Fuck you, Starshine!"

Cats.

THIRTY-TWO

The First Beast was in love. He was in love with a beautifully crafted thing of antiquity. The wooden frame carved by the hands of time, was grown from the very trees of Eden. Its cushions were covered with leathers of the men killed in battle by Ares, the god of war. It was adorned with magnificent pearls and a Golden Fleece hung over one of the armrests. Rose petals were scattered all around it from the First Beast's many attempts in wooing said piece of furniture. However, she didn't say much and his pursuits were always ignored. The First Beast was in love with a sofa that didn't, and couldn't, love him back. So he did what many do with unrequited love. He drank the pain away.

It was morning and his seven heads were pounding. He was riddled with anxiety about the night before. *Did I make a fool of myself? I was just having a good time. Was it my scar? Did she think my horns were silly?* The First Beast, while having seven heads, only had ten horns, which didn't make for a very even distribution.

He stood up and went to get some water. It wasn't working for him. *Maybe I need to taper off a bit.* No one wants to just dive into a hangover. The First Beast certainly didn't want that. However, he had the paws of a bear and making a Bloody Mary wasn't easy with bear paws. He walked over to the corner. His lair was made up of the different seasons, one for each corner. He liked the spring corner the most; however the winter corner was perfect for keeping the booze cold.

He clamped an empty glass and scooped up some slush. He added some vodka, tossed in some tomato juice and introduced a celery stick to his breakfast.

He was the First Beast, and he had seven heads of seven lions, all in sync with one another. He had the body of a leopard and the paws of a bear. There were golden crowns on his unevenly horned heads, with one head larger than others in the middle and having a huge scar down the side of it. He was created for the future and one day his fate will be revealed when he rises from the sea to bring on the end times of man. His power will be undeniable and he will reign destruction down on earth. He also loves Grey's Anatomy and is part of the quiet minority that enjoyed the musical episode.

He was born into darkness at the beginning of the fall of man, but like most living beings, he doesn't remember it. He just kind of remembers being, but he will always remember meeting her. It was during a midnight stroll through the deserts of Calcem, the Heel of Hell. She was shining in the moonlight on the field of an ancient battle. It was in love at first sight, and he chivalrously carried his bae back to his lair.

The booze cleared him up a little bit, and his headache began to settle.

"We have to talk," he said quietly to his love.

She did not respond.

He sighed. "I feel like the spark just isn't here anymore. I'm the only one trying in this relationship."

Again silence, because she was a fucking sofa.

"Is it my scar?" He took a big gulp and refilled his glass. "I just need you. I can't keep going on this way." He was starting to slur his speech.

"SAY SOMETHING DAMMIT! HOW CAN YOU BE SO CRUEL?"

They were interrupted by the door to their lair opening. Although she was just a sofa, one could almost feel her relief.

The Second Beast walked through the door. His two curved horns wrapped around like a ram. He walked like a man and was wearing a dark robe. The plants in the summer and spring corners wilted. The snow in the winter corner began to melt. The First Beast towered above him.

"I need you to do something," the Second Beast hissed.

"I'm in no shape for work; I'm a broken man..," the First Beast slurred as he lie down in heartbroken defeat.

"She's still giving you the silent treatment?" hissed the Second Beast.

"It's over. I have no more energy."

"Stop talking that way, man. You guys will get through this. No relationship is without its ups and downs." He walked over to console his friend.

"You know I'm here for you man...but right now I need your help. I've just been told that the Watcher kid is down here and he isn't alone. He has some suicide from Capite with him, and they are getting closer to finding Jack. This is spiraling out of control, and I'm afraid that if he keeps going, all of the condemned are going to see it… Look, I may have the horns, but they have the numbers. We need to keep this thing quiet. Get it?" The Second Beast patted him on the back.

"What about Hank? Isn't this his job?" The First Beast said through muffles of one of his heads hidden in his elbow.

"This is too important for that stupid camel. We never should have given him wings. He's a dick."

"I'm just so empty inside. I don't think I will be any good." He sniffled, his great bear paws wiping away a tear.

"Hey there.." The Second Beast looked at him. "Don't let what he wants eclipse what you need. He's very dreamy, but he's not the sun. You are."

"Cristina Yang, Season 10 Episode 24," the First Beast said with his last sniffle as he looked back as his friend. He collected himself and stood up. "Okay, I'm in. I'll take care of the Watcher and his friends."

THIRTY-THREE

The pathway that led from the iron gates was large and well lit from an assortment of torches against the rocky walls. The floors were no longer the damp, musty carpet like they were on the path from Capite. It was a polished marble that reflected Colin and Wade as they hurriedly scrambled down the path, fearful of being found. Their steps echoed throughout the emptiness as they ran toward a large double door at the end of the gigantic corridor. Colin could make out the writing above it.

QUIET PLEASE. COURT IN SESSION.

"What do you suppose goes on in here?" Colin asked even though he already knew the answer.

Wade took hold of the iron door handle and began to pull it open very slowly. Inside was a large red lit courtroom with a crowd of hundreds of demons gathered around a smaller central floor. It resembled an auditorium. They were on the top looking down at the rows of seats before hiding behind a massive pillar. They poked their heads around to see what the commotion was.

In the middle of the room, beneath the surrounding

bleacher seats of tortured souls, was a young man in his mid thirties. He was wearing a nice buttoned down shirt and tie, with well tailored black pants. His hands were bound by old rusted chains, and a little tiny demon was tickling his nose with a feather. The man sneezed before the judge entered the room.

"All rise for the evil, yet honorable, Judge Marcus Washington," the bailiff bellowed.

The demons stood up and quieted down.

"Have a seat," the judge said as he motioned to everyone. He loved the whole process. The bailiff was an actual bailiff in his life on earth and followed the procedure wonderfully.

"Christopher Clark, welcome to the darkest darkness th..," the judge began.

"Present, Your Honor," the man said with a slow Missouri accent.

"You don't have to say 'present.' I was just beginning to get into my thing."

"Oh sorry…"

"Christopher Clark, welcom…"

"Yes?"

"No, you don't have to say anything, that's just how I like to begin these things. Just shut up and listen, okay?"

"Christopher Cla….oh dammit. Now it just feels forced. Look, you are here because you have been a total bag of dickery with your life on earth. Do you agree with this?"

The man just stood there in silence.

"You can say something now," the judge said, with a frustrated tone in his voice.

"Oh sorry…"

"Do you agree?"

"With what?"

"That you've been a total bag of dickery in life?"
"What's that mean?"
"It's a common colloquialism."
"I've never heard it before."
"That doesn't matter. It's very common. Just answer the question."

"Well I can't rightly give an answer if I don't know what the question means can I? I mean, I can probably infer the definition, given your not-so-subtle inflictions of prejudice, but what if I'm wrong? The art of conversation relies heavily on clarity of communication. If we can't fully appreciate each other's meanings, then I fear that we've lost before we've started. "

"Bailiff, you've heard that phrase right?" the judge asked as he looked over to the large demon in a security guard suit.

"What's that, Your Honor?" the bailiff responded.

"A bag of dickery," the judge responded.

"Oh sure, sure I've heard that before," the bailiff reassured His Honor.

"See?" The judge said to Christopher.

"Well, come to think of it, I've only really heard you use it, Your Honor," the bailiff retold the judge.

"I second that," Christopher added.

"It's a common term. Whatever, let's just move past it," the judge said to them both.

"Well, if it's the reason I'm being condemned to eternal damnation, I'd like to know what it means," Christopher protested.

"No, it's not the reason you… well it is the reason. If you knew what it meant it would make sense…," the judge sighed in frustration. "Okay, so if you had to guess, why would you say you are here?"

"Oh, probably because of all those people I

scammed."

"That's correct. What do you…"

"I mean 'allegedly' scammed."

"Allegedly..? No. Your soul is in Hell, we already know exactly what you did down here."

"Well then why are you asking me?"

"It's part of the process. The pageantry is important. Dammit, look…we know you stole millions of dollars from old women all around the world. We know all about your Blockbuster video scams. We know about your life insurance fraud."

"ALLEGED Blockbuster Video scams."

"NO. NO. Not 'alleged.' We KNOW what happened. You called up old women and told them their movies were overdue and they owed thousands of dollars."

"Well, I'd rather not self incriminate myself. I plead the fifth, Your Honor."

"What? No…you're already guilty."

"I don't get a trial?!"

"No!"

"Am I at least guaranteed some form of representation?"

"No!!"

"That's not fair."

"This is Hell. It's not supposed to be fair."

"Well, what about the goodhearted nature of the many acts of kindness performed by yours truly? A couple of bad deeds can sentence me to an eternity of torment? What about that time I employed a homeless woman? She needed help and I helped her. If that doesn't qualify as a bona fide act of Jesus, then I suppose that we do indeed live ambivalent lives in an apathetic world where nothing matters. How come that wasn't acknowledged?"

"You stole her social security number and used her

identity to buy a jet ski."

"I let her ride it!"

"No. Nothing you did in life will help balance out the bad. It's too late. We are going to move on to the sentencing."

"Well, if you would just take into account…"

"No if's about it. We're moving on."

"Well, if you would just listen…"

"No more if's pal. IF a bullfrog had wings he wouldn't bump his ass when he hopped." The judge looked around the courtroom beaming with pride.

"What the hell does a flying bullfrog have to do with anything?"

"Oh, come on! It's another common colloquialism."

"I've never heard it."

"It's a very common saying."

"Yeah I'm not familiar with that one either, Your Honor," the bailiff mentioned.

"If a bullfrog had wings then the mere act of hopping would seem futile at best and downright criminal at worst, would it not? You had better use what the good Lord gave you, am I right? Never waste a gift." Christopher said, nodding to the crowd.

The crowd nodded in agreement.

"No, that's not what that phrase means. It just means that 'if' doesn't matter..," The judge tried to explain.

"Oh wait….I get it. If a bullfrog 'ALLEGEDLY' had wings…."

"No…"

"I think it means that the wings would help cushion the bullfrog's ass when it lands," the bailiff added.

"Oh, I see, so it's more of some sort of evolutionary parachute system designed as a safety measure for the high impact nature of a bullfrog's hop," Christopher said.

"No. That's not what I'm saying." The judge began to turn red.

"It's because a bullfrog needs wings to help them catch the flies!" a demon shouted from the crowd.

"Oh, that makes sense," the bailiff said as he nodded.

"Actually, bullfrogs have been known to jump upwards of six feet, and being the ambush predators they are, often sit motionless using the factor of surprise to capture their prey. So wings would have been a waste of the evolutionary process." Christopher corrected.

"Ohhh..," the crowd murmured with interest.

The judge paused for a moment to collect himself. He was losing control of the room. He breathed in deeply.

"Christopher Clark, I hereby senten…."

"Yes?"

"Fuck it. I can't do this anymore." The judge threw his hands in the air. "Put him in the cobra pit. This court is adjourned." He slammed down the gavel and walked out.

The demons erupted in a chorus of cheers. Two guards grabbed Christopher by the shoulders and dragged him out of the courtroom. They exited out of a wooden door behind the podium in which the judge sat.

*   *   *   *   *

The demons began to disband and leave throughout the many exits at the top of the stadium seating. Colin and Wade hid in the shadows until the room was empty.

"That must have been where they took Jack," Colin said, pointing at the same door the poor bag of dickery was taken through moments before.

"I wonder what else we'll see down here," Wade said under his breath.

"Besides an old man getting his balls lit up like a

Christmas tree or a flying demon camel?"

"It's been a day."

"Well, we can't quit now. How are we going to find out where they sent Jack?"

The two looked around court.

"There must be some sort of record keeping maybe? Right?" Colin asked.

"There," Wade said, pointing his gnarled finger toward the stenograph machine next to the judge's podium. "Maybe we can trace back to Jack's sentencing."

"It's worth a shot," Colin answered as he walked toward the machine.

It was an antique, an elegant shorthand typewriter. The keys were rusted. The paper was frail. There was an iron bucket next to the table filled to the rim with the paper rolls. There were months and months of courtroom minutes recorded for who knows what.

Colin began to sift through the paper searching for signs of Jack's court appearance. Finally, he found something. He read:

Jack Charlton – Nope. Not what I said. You must be hearing things. Are you sure you're feline okay?

Judge Marcus Washington - Jack Charlton you are hereby sentenced to eternity in cell 333. TAKE HIM AWAY.

Jack Charlton - Real quick, what's the weed situation down here? Are we all pretty cool or what?

"This is Jack for sure. Looks like he's in cell 333. Well that's a start. It also looks like he's in a room with a bunch of cats," Colin said as he read through the transcript.

"Cats? That doesn't sound so bad," Wade mentioned.

"An eternity with cats is the worst possible thing that could happen to a guy like Jack."

They headed toward the exit in the rear of the room. The door was unlocked and easy to open. They walked through and found themselves on a pathway that looked over a giant pit. The ground was made of old red stone bricks. There were thousands of floors above and below them. At the very top, Colin could make out a starry sky. Deep below them was pure darkness and the sounds of waves crashing against rocks.

"Do we go up or down?"

Colin shrugged and began walking up the spiral pathway. It created a circle along the outside of the pit, much like the threading of a screw. As they passed the first cell they heard quiet laughter and the sound of electricity. Markings above the door read CCC.

"CCC." Wade noticed. "Great…We're looking for cell 333 and we ain't even in the numbers section yet!"

They continued walking. The next door read CCCI, the next one, CCCII.

"These aren't letters," Colin said. "They're Roman numerals. C means one hundred. Three C's….this is room 302! We're going the right way."

They picked up the pace and began a slow jog up the slope.

"V means five. X means ten….We need to find the one marked CCCXXXIII!" Colin said as he calculated the numerals in his head.

They passed by a number of doors, with the sounds of zapping and punching and screaming. Eventually they were there, room CCCXXXIII. There were no windows on the door. Just the quiet murmurs of meows inside.

THIRTY-FOUR

"Fuck it."

Jack was on his back looking at the ceiling as the cats were wandering around on top of him. Some were kneading him. Others were licking his feet.

"I give up. I give in to my punishment. I am in Hell, and this is my nightmare."

One of the cats coughed up a hairball in the corner.

"I don't even care anymore. Maybe I've been wrong my whole life. Maybe you guys are doing it right. I mean, Kevin...look at you. You just shit wherever you want, whenever you want. You are living it right, brother. I have been confined to a box my whole life. A litter box of judgment. 'Get a job.' 'Finish college.' 'Don't get chlamydia.' It's exhausting! Maybe that's why I worked so hard to go against the grain."

Kevin rolled to the ground and batted the air. Darren climbed aboard and lay down on Jack's bare chest.

"Take me away, felines. I'm yours now." Jack said as he accepted his agony. He closed his eyes. He imagined an ocean of cats carrying him off into the yonder, toward a small island made of litter.

"Oh, Hell...how you sting the soul!"

He laid in his defeat.

"You Sting the Soul would have been such a great song title!" he cried out once more. Then he heard knocking.

*   *   *   *   *

Colin was banging on door CCCXXXIII.

"Jack!...Jack are you in there?" he yelled into the wooden planks that made up the cell door. There was no handle on the door; otherwise it would have been furiously wiggled.

Wade shushed him and pointed across the pit. There were two demons making their way down the path. They had not noticed Wade or Colin yet, but eventually they would see them.

"Shit," Colin muttered...he went back to knocking gently. "Jack!" he said in a hushed voice.

"Hello?" Jack muttered back from the other end.

"Jack is it you?!" Colin could barely hold his excitement.

"Who is this?" Jack responded.

"It's Colin...are you okay?! Is there a way to open this door?!"

"Do you think if I knew how to open the door that I wouldn't have opened it yet?"

"Good point. We're here to rescue you...."

"You're doing great, buddy."

"There's no handle. There's no way to open this thing!"

"Really? There's a handle on this side..."

"Have you tried it?"

"Of course I've tried it, do you think..," the door clicked opened.

"Huh?..well what do you know? I guess the door was unlocked the whole time. Talk about frustrating," Jack said as the door slowly swung open.

"Quick let us in!" Wade said as they hurried into the cell, closing the door behind them.

The three of them stood in silence at the door waiting for the demons to patrol past them. They were immediately swarmed by the army of cats. Purrs filled the room as they all took turns rubbing against their legs.

"Wow, that's a lot of cats," Wade commented.

Colin introduced Wade. "Jack, this is Wade. Wade, Jack. Wade killed himself and helped me find you."

"Good to finally meet you," Wade said as they shook hands.

"COLIN!" Jack said as he barreled him up in a giant bear hug. "I'm so happy to see you!"

"Couldn't you have waited to do that until you put your shirt back on?" Colin laughed as he handed his friend his lost shirt.

"Oh you met Lincoln? He's a crusty old fuck, isn't he?"

"He helped us get in here."

"He punched a guy," Wade added.

"Really?" Jack was impressed. "It was probably Tom."

"Yep, them guards zapped his nuts, too."

"We don't know that for sure," Colin said.

"They zapped mine. It's no vacation. I think the dudes are still smoking," Jack said.

"Oh man...I peed on an electric fence once. I can't imagine an actual taser!"

"I'll never roast chestnuts again, I can say..."

"Can we continue this conversation once we're out of here?" Colin interrupted.

"Where do we go now?" Wade asked.

"Well I'm no expert, but I'm assuming the best way to get out of a pit is up," Colin answered.

Wade opened the door slowly and poked his head out. The demons were nowhere to be seen. The coast was clear. Jack kneeled down to the felines.

"Goodbye, my friends. I know we didn't always see eye to eye, but there was real love here. I know that now. Kevin, you stay frosty. Starshine, always follow your dreams. Darren…well, I still don't actually like you, but I appreciate your plight. I know it can't be easy being you. You have a lot of anger built up, and I guess that when I see you, I see myself…and that scares me."

Jack stood up, and the three men darted out the door. They began to run up the spiraling pathway toward the starry sky above. Colin noticed, as they neared the top, that it wasn't a starry sky at all, but holes in the ceiling of an enormous cavern. They reached the top and followed a short pathway out.

The end of the path led onto a grassy field, illuminated by the blue sky poking through the top. The three men trekked on through the grass, unsure of what direction, but sure of the distance they wanted between them and the dungeon pit behind them.

The grass was damp and cold to the touch. It made a sloshing sound with every footstep. Wade's feet were turning red, and they soon realized that the field was soaked in blood. In the distance they began to make out the figures of men on the ground. It was some sort of ancient battlefield. A large hill appeared in the distance and without speaking they continued walking toward it. It was quiet. There were many questions running through each of their minds, but none dared to break the silence.

The ground rumbled.

"Now what?" Colin asked.

THIRTY-FIVE

The ground rumbled again. The three stopped walking and stood still, listening.

"Look at that!" Jack said quietly as he pointed to the top of the hill.

There was an old couch shining in the light. It was elegant with uneven patches of leather stitched together. The three looked at the couch, unsure of their next move.

"I've brought my betrothed here, so that she can witness my victory on this field of battle," A monstrous voice said from behind. The three turned around to see a massive, multi headed beast in standing in full armor.

"Who the hell are you?!" Colin said, trying to hide his panic.

"I am the usher of end times. I am the breaker of men. I am the scourge of the underworld. I am the First Beast of the sea…" The beast stood tall.

"And your betrothed is that couch up there?" Jack asked.

"She is my heart and soul, and I hope to make sweet, poetic love to her after I have devoured you wretched beings. I'm going to stomp you to the ground. This is Calcem, and I am the Heel of Hell!"

The beast began to circle them. The armor was scratched and battle worn. Each head wore a different helmet. The main head in the middle wore a large Viking helmet with a crack down the side that was perfectly aligned with his scar.

"Are you going to eat us or stomp us?" Jack asked again.

"I am going to stomp you...then eat you!" the First Beast declared as he leaped toward them.

The three turned to run. They slipped as they scrambled to get traction. Wade barely rolled out of the way of the beast's might paw. Colin ran off toward the side, but the beast swung one of his heads in front and clotheslined him to the ground. Jack ran to help Colin, but the beast jumped in front, blocking him.

"You will be first!" The monster bellowed.

Jack braced himself.

In the distance there was a loud, whiny meow. They all stopped to look at the hill, the First Beast included. There on the hill was the silhouette of a cat. He sat down and peered down toward the group.

"Darren?!" Jack yelled.

Darren nodded, turned around, and strolled toward the couch. He stretched his back as he began to scratch at the front of the leather cushions. Suddenly, dozens more cats showed up and began to claw the couch. Some lay down to take a nap. Starshine jumped on the back, coughed up a hairball, and then scratched the cushion with a massage like motion.

"MY LOVE! NOOO!" The First Beast yelled in desperation. He began to sprint toward the hill. "I'm coming...don't worry I will save you from these wretched creatures!"

"Fucking Darren..," Jack said with a smile as he

helped Colin to his feet. "We may not like each other, but I'll be damned again if he doesn't remind me of myself sometimes."

The three took off away from the hill. They ran toward some woods in the distance. There was a screech from the sky.

"Jesus...what NOW?!" Colin said, sick of the Hellish rollercoaster he had been on.

"It's Hank! He found us!" Wade said, pointing toward the sky.

"Who's Hank?!" Jack questioned.

"The Demon Camel of Capite." Wade and Colin responded simultaneously.

"A camel?"

The flying camel circled them overhead. His eyes glowed red with an incredible rage. He saw Wade and began to scream again. The ground shook with his landing. He stared at Wade, seething.

"Why is he only looking at me?" Wade asked trembling with fear.

"GOD DAMMIT THAT'S IT!" Jack bellowed. "My girlfriend dumped me for some boring ass square with a nice beard. I have been chased by demons. I have been thrown off of a mountain. I have been trapped with cats in Hell. I have nearly been stomped and devoured by a seven headed monster! There is no fucking way that a stupid flying camel is going to be what does it."

Jack turned to the guys.

"THIS FUCKING CAMEL IS BURNING ME!!"

Jack attacked first. Hank didn't know what to do. He started to back pedal. No one had ever run at him like that before. Jack punched the camel in the face, following it with a brutal headbutt. He grabbed him by the ears and jumped on top. The camel scrambled and took flight, with Jack still on his back. They barreled into the sky, both screaming.

Colin and Wade watched in disbelief as Jack delivered punch after punch into the back of the flying camel's head. He then grabbed him by the ears and guided him back into the ground. They came in too fast for a landing. Jack leapt off of the camel before he crashed and turned to grab him by the head. He stared Hank directly in the eyes.

"YOU ARE GOING TO TAKE MY FRIENDS AND I BACK HOME OR I AM GOING TO BREAK YOUR GODDAMNED HUMPS OFF AND BEAT YOU TO A PULP WITH THEM!!"

The glow in Hank's eyes dimmed as he took in the situation. He bowed down and allowed the songwriter to climb aboard.

"Let's go guys," Jack said calmly to the guys.

"Holy Black Jesus..," Colin said, frozen in disbelief.

He climbed aboard with Jack, and held on to the second hump.

"My friends, I can't come with you," Wade said.

"What are you talking about?" Colin said. "You're in Hell...this is the worst place to be, literally."

"If Jack's door was open, maybe the others are too. I can't leave without trying to help some of those poor souls. I think this is my chance to redeem myself somehow."

Colin understood. Wade was meant for a different path.

"Thanks for your help," Jack said.

"Take care, man." Colin shook his new friend's hand.

Wade nodded and headed back toward the pit. He turned back once more and waved goodbye.

"Let's go, you dick," Jack said, smacking the back of

the camel's head. Hank snorted as they took off and headed through one of the holes in the ceiling.

PART 3

"Well, I told her I was lost
And she told me all about the Pentecost
And I seen that girl as the road to my survival"

- Paul Simon

THIRTY-SIX

BJ clumsily fell to the ground as he pushed open the door to the boiler room. His pride was hurt more than his body, but it quickly vanished when he looked around and saw no one else was there. He quietly shut the door and began to hide behind the large equipment. The room was loud from the machinery and steam blew from various vents. He moved slowly toward the back wall. He needed to get on the elevator.

"Hello?" a voice cut through the steam.

BJ froze in his steps.

"Who dat?" He asked the room.

"Help us. They are breaking into the waiting room. We need to stop them!"

BJ quickly moved through the steam to find Director Hauser and Leah chained to some pipes.

"It's you!" Leah said. "We thought you were gone for good!"

"It's been a hell of a weekend, child," BJ responded.

"Can you free us?" Hauser asked. "There are some bolt cutters in the maintenance closet near the back."

BJ ran to the closet and pulled out the cutters. The chains broke easily under the pressure. Leah stood up and helped the director to his feet.

"Where's Chrissy?" BJ asked.

"Are you talking about the moron who is running this operation?" Leah responded.

"That'd be him."

"He's in the orientation room, I'm assuming he's trying to get the waiting room doors open."

"What's the move?"

"If they can get their army through those doors, there is nothing keeping them from invading Heaven, itself. We have to get up there and make sure those doors stay closed."

"Amorous has an army in the caves. They're about to attack. It's the biggest army I've ever seen."

"Well, we don't have much time then. Let's move." Hauser said.

The elevator dinged as the doors opened. The three walked in and headed to the orientation room.

"He's not going to be alone," Leah said.

"We need fire," BJ said. "Fire sends them back to Hell."

"We don't want fire," Hauser said.

"What?"

"Fire sends the dead to Hell. It doesn't matter where you belong."

"Are you saying...?"

"Fire would send us to Hell, too."

"We don't want fire," BJ agreed.

He and Colin had been lucky, and they didn't even know it. One accidental burn and they would have been banished to heck.

"Is there anything that sends us to Heaven?"

"God?" Hauser answered.

"Speaking of His Holiness....where the hell is he?" BJ

questioned. "You know, we could use some omnipotent help at the moment."

"That isn't how it works."

"Yeah yeah, I've heard it." BJ brushed it off. "I just figured maybe he'd take an interest in the Duke of Hell plotting to take over his kingdom of paradise."

"Maybe he already knows that everything is going to work out okay."

"Oh good, a paradox," BJ said.

*   *   *   *   *

Amauros walked smoothly to the front of the army. Thousands of demons were lined up, waiting for the orders. They were to attack Limbo with everything they got and move in waves into the waiting room where they could overpower the gates to Heaven and finally break through.

The plan went off the rails when Chrissy failed to take his brother's place in secret. Now they were improvising. With Chrissy at the doors and the Rocky Mountain Division acting as a jail, it shouldn't be too much of a detriment. All they had to do is get into that room before the angels stop them.

"Creatures of darkness, bags of dickery alike…this is our moment!" Amauros shouted to his army.

"We have a chance to change our fate and take our piece of pie!"

The demons all cheered. They loved pie. Obviously there is pie in Heaven.

"Get in there and get through that door! ATTACK!"

The army bolted out of the caves and into the sunlight. They darted full speed toward the building, splitting off into different sub groups to attack at different points.

   * * * * *

The elevator opened, and the three exited into the hallway of the top floor of the Rocky Mountain Division. The hallway was dark and quiet.

"With everyone trapped in their rooms, no one has been able to get the mainline power back on." Hauser said softly.

"Is that a good thing?" BJ asked

"We're running on backup generators. The mainline is what controls the main systems, like the security doors..," Hauser answered.

"Like the door to the waiting room," Leah added.

"So that's what he's trying to do, get the power back on," BJ understood.

"If they're trying to get into that room, then that's the only way," Hauser answered.

They continued down the hallway and made their way to the orientation room. They walked in to find Chrissy reclining on a chair near the waiting room. The jogging suit had begun to rip a little bit at the sleeves. He was reading a magazine and didn't notice the three of them walk in.

"Chrissy!" BJ shouted.

It startled the twin brother, and he dropped his magazine.

"OH HELL NO!" he shouted when he saw his brother.

"You're a shitty brother, you know that?" BJ said as they began walking toward them. There was no one else in the room.

"You were so busy up your own ass to even know!"

Chrissy stuttered. "I was a great brother to you!"

"You killed me!"

"You killed me!!"

Chrissy walked around the other side of one of the computer tables, placing it between himself and his brother. In his human form he wasn't nearly as menacing, and he knew it wouldn't be as easy of a fight.

"It's too late, BJ. The power will be back on any minute. Amauros will send his army soon, and Heaven will be ours."

BJ walked around the table, his twin brother mirrored his move.

"What about all of these innocent people?"

"What about them?!" Chrissy snarled. "Why are they so much more innocent than me? One bad mistake is enough to sentence me to an eternity in Hell?! Do you know what I was doing? Before Amauros recruited me? Sponge baths! Not receiving them, either…"

"Look, I know you don't deserve it. I've seen you do good things. I've seen you have good intentions…but there's no changing what happened. These people in here have made mistakes, too. They don't deserve to suffer."

"What do you know?! You've always been spoiled. You've always been the 'golden' child. You didn't deserve this afterlife!" Chrissy began to slow down, his anger was consuming him.

"I'm sorry for the way I treated you. I can see now that I was arrogant. I had an ego. Groupies can do that to a man..," BJ continued, "but you have a chance now to redeem everything you've done. You can still do the right thing. Help us protect this door!"

"This is my chance, you idiot! There's no other choice for me! I get into Heaven and I'm never gonna be that stupid creature again. It changes everything, BJ. It gets into my brain. It makes my thoughts move slower! I can't go back to that. And all that hair…? Nasty, man!"

"Everyone in this waiting room, everyone locked in their rooms here in Limbo, will be sent to Hell! You would do that? Because that is exactly what's going to happen!"

"What? I'm just doing what I'm told."

"You're being used!"

"No…there's room for us all in Heaven. There has to be..," Chrissy said unsurely.

BJ ran toward his brother, but Chrissy was stronger and laid BJ out with one ferocious punch to the head. BJ hit the ground hard, but stood back up and tackled his twin to the ground. Hauser and Leah ran to help, but before they got to the fight, the lights turned back on and the computers buzzed to life.

"The power is back..," Leah said.

The brothers froze with their limbs locked together in a sort of jazzy pretzel. The door to the waiting room opened.

THIRTY-SEVEN

As the sky began to change, Colin could feel the air of Limbo through his hair. He looked at the ground below them and noticed the grass becoming greener. They had been flying for what seemed like half an hour. It amazed Colin to think that the journey between Heaven and Hell was so quick and easy by flight, and so treacherous and maddening by foot.

"We're close," Colin said to Jack, who had been holding Hank by the ears to secure our safe return.

They were coming upon a mountain range in the distance. It resembled the Rockies. Jack looked at them longingly.

"So I was thinking about it back in my cell..," Jack started, "are we like poltergeists then?"

"Isn't a poltergeist like a ghost that's haunting a house?" Colin questioned back.

"I don't know."

"I don't think we're poltergeists, man."

"I'm still going with zombie."

"We're not zombies."

"What are we?"

"Well, when you think about it, we are just in a

different dimension, maybe…"

"So…we're aliens?"

Colin thought about it.

"Maybe?" he said.

"That'd be a huge disappointment compared to being a poltergeist."

Hank made a slight adjustment and began to descend slowly.

"What's it like? Will I be able to hike again?" Jack asked.

"Well…it's a lot of work being a Watcher. You are watching over your client always. It's a job..," Colin could sense Jack's fears. "But once your shift is over and you have helped your client get through their life, well Heaven is just around the corner, and I've heard great things! There's time for everything and everywhere. All of life is at your fingertips."

"I wonder what's going to happen with me once this is all said and done."

Colin was wondering the same thing. Jack didn't deserve to die. It was a freak occurrence. He sure didn't deserve to be sent to Hell. It was just some stupid glitch in the system, but now the system is broken. *How do we come back from that?*

"Whatever happens, I've got your back." Colin felt silly using the phrase, but he wasn't sure how else to word it. They had been through too much together for him to abandon Jack to the fates of whatever else the afterlife had in store for him.

They neared the mountains and felt Hank shift as he maneuvered through the peaks. There was freshness to the air and light clouds all around.

They cleared the peaks and saw the Rocky Mountain Division ahead. The enormous compound looked like a model building from their altitude. As they neared they saw the demonic army moving through the fields. There was already a group breaking into the door. A hooded figure was gliding through from the rear of the attack.

"Colin! We're too late!" Jack panicked.

Colin didn't have time to answer before the sky lit up with thousands of angels breaking through the Heavens above. The sudden flash sent Hank into a tailspin, and the Watchers lost control. Colin could make out the battle beginning through the slow spin. The angels were on top of the demons so quickly that the front wave of the army didn't have time to react. The rest of the demons scattered. Amauros stood still and made a motion toward the caves. Another force of demons entered the field from the dark entrance, each holding long spears with flames on the end. They spread out at the rear of the attack and held the spears toward the sky. An angel flew from the back end and in a glorious effort to send one of them back to Hell, he swooped. The demon made a swift move with the spear and connected with the angel. In a flash the angel vanished, leaving only white feathers from the wings.

"Oh!" Colin cried out, but was silenced as the demon camel of Capite hit the ground face-first, sending Jack and his rescuer tumbling.

Jack stood up with his hands out as if he was surfing and collected his balance. He was always just athletic enough to piss off his musician friends. Colin landed a few feet away, face down. Jack rolled Colin over, grabbed him by the arm and lifted him to his feet.

"What now?!" Jack questioned.

They were in the heat of the battle, with demons running in all directions. Every few moments one of them got tossed into oblivion by an angel.

"Where's Hank?!" Colin asked.

Jack looked around before pointing toward the cave. There he saw the backend of the most cowardly demon camel Capite had to offer, running away at a full sprint.

"THIS ISN'T OVER!" Jack screamed at the AWOL dromedary. "I'LL FIND YOU, YOU SON OF A BITCH!"

The two kept moving through the battle. A large demon saw the two of them and charged toward them. He had a large branch he was using as a weapon. Colin froze as he saw the monster near him, with the weapon held back like a baseball bat. An angel appeared out of nowhere and snagged the demon before he could connect.

The battle was raging. The field was full of yells and growls from the demons and the booming sounds of the voiceless angels' wings. They could see the division in the distance.

"We have to find BJ!" Colin shouted. "We have to get to the waiting room!"

The two ran toward the building. The demons were preoccupied with avoiding the angels and reaching the building themselves. They barely took notice of the two men racing along with them.

*   *   *   *   *

In the rear of the field, the flaming-spear wielding demons were maneuvering their weapons with the pageantry of flag girls on acid. For having an eternity to train, Amauros found no need for it. *What is so difficult about poking something with a stick?* He would think.

One demon found it especially difficult and couldn't seem to find the balance between swinging and poking.

In his past life, he worked in a computer store. He was soft-spoken and reserved, had never played sports as a kid, and didn't have much of a competitive nature. Apathy and wistfulness were his strongest traits. In fact, one of the biggest sins he had ever committed was doing absolutely nothing with his life. Oh, and he murdered hitchhikers.

Customers called him Brent. His name was Brett. He never bothered to correct them.

It was on a sunny afternoon that Brett decided to do something he had only dreamed of. He was going to go skydiving. It was something that he had in his heart as a small boy. The idea of flying through the sky and feeling the air through his thinning hair would be his moment. It seemed like a way to wake himself up and start living his life.

He paid the fee and signed the waiver and sat through the safety video. There were other, gnarlier dudes and dudettes along with him. However, as usual he didn't fit in, but this time he didn't even notice. He was committed to the jump. He was ready to fly.

The airplane was small, and the man he was attached to was large. He felt safe tandem jumping with this guy. Brett wore him like a third grader with a new backpack.

The light went off and it was time to fly. Brett's heart was racing for the first time since he could remember. They approached the door, and the instructor was yelling something, but Brett wasn't listening. It was loud. Before Brett had time to take in the moment, they were out the door.

It was incredible. The world was so big in front of him. He was seeing true beauty for the first time. He vowed to never hurt another hitchhiker again. He was changed.

He began to notice the instructor jerking at the pull cord in frenzy. Something was wrong. Brett's heart began to sink. This wasn't good. The parachute was malfunctioning. He pulled the secondary chute. It released only for them to see the gaping hole in it, the fabric tearing up with the velocity.

What was to be Brett's new beginning turned out to be his end. They were plummeting toward Earth and they were both going to die. The instructor grabbed Brett and rotated their bodies, placing himself behind. *He's using me to soften the landing!* Brett's panic turned into complete fear.

They landed hard. Brett didn't even feel it. He was dead from a heart attack seconds before impact. The instructor walked away with barely a limp. He, too, eventually went to Hell.

Brett was watching the sky for angels, holding his flaming spear out in front of him. Out of the side an angel flew into him swooping him up into the sky. They struggled as the angel climbed higher. In an instant, Brett positioned the flames into the angel's wings sending him into the void with a flash. This sent Brett flailing through the sky.

He was having flashbacks of his death as he flew into the fifth story windows of the division. The flaming spear followed and landed on some beautifully woven curtains. They caught flame. Brett stood up and found himself surrounded by the burning room. *Well shit.* He thought, as the flames engulfed him and sent him back to Hell.

The fire spread from the room and into the hall. With the division locked down, there was no one available to help stop the inferno. It moved easily. The Rocky Mountain Division was on fire.

Thirty-Eight

Chrissy let out a yell as BJ bit into his arm. The twins had rolled into the newly opened waiting room and were wrestling throughout the surprised commotion of bored souls waiting on their number to be called.

Chrissy rolled onto his back and kicked his brother off of him. BJ landed on his back, and the two laid on the floor, feet to feet.

Director Hauser and Leah looked at the doors of the orientation room to see the demons begin to enter. They spread out and began to surround the two of them. They approached the waiting room doors, slowly turning back into their human form as they walked through.

"Chrissy, these people do not deserve this. The demons had their chances. Taking over Heaven…it's not right."

"You think I deserve to be in Hell?! Your own brother?!" Chrissy hissed.

The demons stood still, unsure of their next move. One woman stood from her chair in the waiting room and began to run away in fear. She was struck down by one of the demons, who then looked around cautiously.

The room erupted into chaos. The demons began

beating the people waiting on their turn to enter Heaven. They were being dragged away.

Chrissy stood silently and watched everything unfold.

Director Hauser was fighting off one of the creatures when another one hit him in the back with a chair. He dropped to the ground. Three creatures picked him up and threw him into the hall. Leah was helping a group of people escape through the opposite wall and into the stairwell.

Smoke began to fill the orientation room. The fire was getting closer. Most folks didn't notice.

* * * * *

Colin and Jack bolted into the stairwell. The slam of the door bounced off of the concrete floors and echoed throughout. Smoke followed them as they darted up the stairs, taking them two at a time.

"It's this way!" Colin yelled back to Jack.

A demon crashed through the doors onto the floor above them. He was holding a baseball bat and was cursing to himself in some unknown language. Colin couldn't understand it, but could tell he was grumpy. Flames peaked out from behind him. The fire was growing.

He saw the two of them below and turned to block their path. Colin and Jack spun around to head back down the stairs, but the fire had blocked them in. They were trapped. The demon began to step toward them, bouncing the bat off of the metal handrails.

"Shaka laka Moomba jumba!" The demon hissed at them.

"What the hell is he saying?" Colin thought out loud.

"I think he wants a handjob," Jack mentioned. "Not

it!"

The demon continued toward them, with eyes burning red. The stairs below began to crack. The demon froze and looked down. As the stairs crumbled below him, Colin watched as the demon slipped through into the flames and disappeared with a flash, leaving the bat bouncing on the concrete stairs. Colin picked it up before it rolled into the flames.

They jumped over the hole, before the fire continued to eat the rest of the stairs, and headed toward the orientation room.

*   *   *   *   *

"I'm sorry for the way I treated you. I can see now that I was arrogant. I had an ego. Groupies can do that to a man..." BJ stood up. *"But you have a chance now to redeem everything you've done. You can still do the right thing. Help us protect this door!"*

Chrissy looked at his brother and remembered what he had said. He felt something he hadn't felt in a long time. It was a sense of humanity.

The flames peaked through the orientation room doors as more demons flooded the room. Soon the waiting room would be overrun and all that stood between Heaven and Hell would be a relatively small white gate.

The demons began throwing people into the flames and laughing as they disappeared in a flash of light. Chrissy saw the fear in a young man's eyes as he was dragged across the floor and thrown into a burning table.

The demon was laughing before being smashed in the back of the head by a baseball bat. Colin stood over him as Jack used his legs to push the fallen creature into the flames. They had ducked into the orientation room through the back stairs, and were making their way toward the waiting room. The demons focused their attention on the two new arrivals and began to surround them. Colin held the bat up ready to defend himself. Jack put up his fists not willing to go down without a fight.

Seeing Colin again was all Chrissy needed to realize that maybe he was being used. Colin shouldn't have been taken the way he was, and the blood was on Chrissy's hands.

He didn't have time to question the paradox of sin. He didn't think on the philosophy of good and bad on a cosmic scale. He only knew that what he was doing felt wrong, and he wouldn't be able to go on without doing something to make it right.

"Chrissy!" BJ was yelling, now on his feet trying to help people escape the craziness.

Chrissy looked back at his brother. BJ stood still and watched his twin brother turn back toward the orientation room and charge the demons.

As he ran through the doors, back into the orientation room, Chrissy slowly began to change back into his gorilla like form. He smashed through tables and handed out haymakers like candy. He approached the demons, tossing them into the surrounded flames like he was dusting an old shelf. Colin watched as the monster grabbed the demons that surrounded him with an enormous bear hug. He caught eyes with Colin, and with the same fury that Colin had seen when he was killed, Chrissy dove into the burning heap of computers and tables, taking the small force of demons with him. In a flash, they were gone. Colin and Jack were saved.

"It's BJ!" Jack grabbed Colin by the shoulders and pointed. The waiting room was still under attack and despite Chrissy's heroic efforts there wasn't much left they could do.

The creatures made it to the white gates. They were shaking it and beating it with chairs. It couldn't hold much longer.

The windows crashed open to the angels breaking through. They began to fight off the demons, sending them flying through walls and smashing through the floors. The souls of the waiting room were escaping through the holes and fighting back the best they could. It was too late.

The gates broke open and the white light of Heaven began to shine through. Everyone was blinded for a moment. Then, in a stampede of the blessed and cursed, everyone charged the door.

"No..," Colin whispered to himself.

The three of them watched as everyone invaded Heaven. They didn't notice Amauros walk into the room.

THIRTY-NINE

The fluffy dog grunted as he landed. It was a short jump from a small mound, but the ground was hard and he was bored. It was a hot day in the deep forest somewhere in what we call Mississippi today, but at this time, this land was uncharted and unnamed.

He sniffed the air and moved quietly into the trees ahead and scanned the surroundings. It was silent. He froze.

Minutes passed until he heard a small snap of a twig. The labradoodle turned his head toward the sound and saw the fox looking back at him, his leg in midair, motionless from the surprise. The fox took off with the designer breed in tow.

Leaves rustled and birds took flight as the two darted through the woods. They had been pursuing each other for many, many years. The race began in Greece, and since then it has covered all parts of the world.

The fox jumped into a tree and called back to the dog.

"How long have I been evading you?" the fox asked whimsically.

"Time is irrelevant. It's not about time, it's about the capture," The labradoodle answered as he walked toward the tree. He circled three times and lay down. The fox let his tail hang and rested on the branch.

"I'm growing tired of this. It's obvious there will be no end. I have been thinking of a new game," the fox said nonchalantly.

*   *   *   *   *

It all escalated in the Garden of Eden. The devil's fall from grace would begin with a game. He would approach the Lord with questions.

"Lord?" Lucifer would ask. "If you can do all things, could you create something that even you could not destroy?"

"Of course," God would answer. "However, I am not to be tested."

"Oh it wouldn't be a test…I just want to witness your omnipotent glory."

"Look around you," The Lord would say as he motioned to his newly created world. "Isn't this enough? We can do so much here. We can spread so much love."

"You have too many rules. Love should be without bounds. We should be able to bang it out with whomever we want, whenever we want."

"You don't understand what makes love so incredible, Luc," God would explain.

"You have too much loss. Time should be endless. People shouldn't have limits. Fuck that shit."

"You would then only take away the beauty of a moment. Life is made up of moments."

"You have too much suffering. These people will learn to hate you for their pain. I wouldn't have created suffering."

"There is no strength without suffering, Devil. Life

cannot work without balance. Their pain will end when they join us in Heaven. That is the prize for living a worthy life."

"Well if you can do ALL THINGS, then WHY does it need to be this way?"

God turned toward the Devil, and they looked into each other's eyes.

"I know why you question me. You're always nagging me. I know it was you who destroyed the dinosaurs. I know you want to betray me. I know you want to go your own way. The world needs balance, but I don't want you here anymore."

Lucifer was angry at this. He wore the white robes of the angels, but carried a heavier heart than them. He hated just standing idle while the Lord was stifling a damned near perfect way of life. And he wasn't alone. He had many other angels that agreed with him. They would spend their time on the outskirts of Heaven drinking and talking philosophy. They would offer ideas of what they would do differently. They would cheer Lucifer on and feed his ego. He began to believe he could do a better job in the boss's chair.

"You can't banish me from this place. I have done nothing but help you and follow every order you have given!" He was angry.

"I know what's in your heart! You have been talking with the girls in the garden. You are trying to poison their minds."

"I'm trying to free their minds!"

"You're trying to betray me!" The Lord was angry.

"It's not all about you!" Lucifer was losing control.

"You are not to set foot on this world again." The clouds began to darken and the Lord had begun to glow.

"Let me have one challenge..," Lucifer asked quietly.

"If you win, then I will never return. If I win...then this world will belong to me."

"You would challenge me right now? When I'm this pissed at you?!"

"You are the Alpha and the Omega, right? The balls? Why would you be afraid of a tiny challenge? It's a simple task for the eternal powers of God."

The Lord stood in silence, waiting for him to finish.

" You...who can do ALL things...I'm talking anything at all..."

"Yes?"

"Could you create a fox that could never be caught?"

"Of course I could."

"Then could you, yourself, catch this 'uncatchable' fox?"

"Yes I could."

"Then it wouldn't be 'uncatchable' would it?"

"What is your challenge, Luc?"

"I want you to do the undoable. Then I will leave quietly."

The Lord smiled at this. He liked games. This was one of the reasons he created dating. He thought for a moment and then calmed down. The clouds went away and the sun shone through.

"Okay, I'm game, but YOU will be the uncatchable fox, and I will be the hound that catches all things. I'll accept this challenge. The game is afoot, motherfucker."

With that a small red fox appeared from the woods and trotted over to the devil's feet. He looked up to find that the Lord still standing there, but a labradoodle was sitting at his feet. The animals circled each other before the dog spoke.

"What are the rules, Devil?" the labradoodle asked.

"Run," the fox answered before darting into the

garden.

The dog howled into the sunshine and chased after.

*   *   *   *   *

The afternoon was dragging on. The humidity was getting thicker.

"We've been at this chase, off and on, for so long, dude." the fox said as he jumped from his branch and stepped toward the resting dog.

"Soon you will understand how it all works," the dog answered, rolling on his back and showing his belly to the sky. "Besides, this was your idea, remember?"

"Well I may have another idea."

He walked over and lay down next to the dog. He rolled over in the same fashion, belly to the sky.

"Of all the creations, the sky may be my favorite." the fox admitted.

"Spoken like someone who lives in a pit," the dog mentioned pretentiously.

"Spoken like someone…who is a dickpuppet," the fox fired back.

"Spoken like a criminal," the dog breathed.

"Spoken like a……." the fox was so angry he couldn't think "chode…uh….wiz..ard! A chode-wizard!"

The dog remained silent.

They relaxed in the wet grass for a bit, staring into the blue above them.

"What is this other 'game' you were talking about?" the dog asked.

"Well, the Lord can do all things right? I'm talking ALL THINGS here..," Fox responded.

"This again? Yes…of course."

"I still haven't been caught, you know?"

"Soon you will understand. What is your question?"

"Can the all powerful and omnipotent Lord… who can do ALL things….with no bounds… create a door that could never be opened even by him?"

"Of course," the lazy dog answered. The clouds slowed in the sky.

"I'll believe it when I see it."

The fox jumped up and darted back into the woods. The labradoodle stood up, shook off the dew, and continued the chase.

FORTY

Amauros moved slowly into the burning orientation room. Colin and Jack had their backs to him as they watched the chaos unfold in the waiting room. They didn't hear him until he spoke.

"So we finally meet," Amauros said. He couldn't see the shock on their faces as they spun around.

Colin and Jack locked into the Duke of Hell's blackened eyes, unsure of what to say. BJ joined them from where he was standing. He was still processing his brother's change of heart. Chrissy had sacrificed himself to save the innocent folks in the waiting room, but it looked like it was all in vain.

"You've been quite the pain, Colin," Amauros said to the Watcher.

"How do you know my name? Who are you?" Colin questioned back.

"I have been planning this ever since that stupid twin brother of his fell into my lap. It was just by fate alone that you were Donald's client," Amauros mentioned.

"Donald? Who's Donald?" Colin was confused.

"Me," BJ admitted.

"What?" Colin asked. "Well what the does the BJ

stand for?"

"I think I know," Jack said.

Jack was ignored.

BJ looked at Colin with surprise.

"Big Juicy, motherfucka," BJ/Donald revealed.

"Nope, I was wrong. I was thinking of something else," Jack stated.

"You think you know somebody," Colin focused back to the shrouded Duke of Hell.

"So this was your entire plan? You had me killed. You sent these creatures after Jack. For what?! To break into Heaven? Where's the endgame here, man?"

"Hell isn't big enough for me!" Amauros answered. He pulled his hood down and revealed his pale, wrinkled face. There was thin white hair covering the top of his head, with a widow's peak down the forehead. His robe dragged across the floor as he moved closer. His hands held out to guide him.

"Wait, can you see, dude?" Jack asked the duke.

"I haven't needed sight for a very long time. I'm used to the darkness. I am one with…"

BAM!

Amauros stumbled backwards from the computer keyboard Jack had thrown. It had hit him square in the face and the impact left him dazed. The three men took off running into the burning halls of the Rocky Mountain Division. Amauros let out a booming roar behind them.

They hustled through the smoky halls and slid as they turned to get down the stairwell.

"We need to get outside!" Colin yelled. "We can't dodge these flames forever!"

As they ran down the stairwell, BJ kept looking behind them. There was no sign of Amauros, but it didn't feel safe. They kept moving.

The doors flew open and the smoke bellowed out. The three men came out of the building clearing the air with their hands. The army had diminished, with the occasional demon in the distance being pursued by an angel.

"Everyone is either in Heaven or Hell! There's no one left in Limbo!" Colin panicked.

They watched as the division burned. The flaming complex towered above them. BJ couldn't help but feel a wave of sadness. This had been his home for a long time.

"Where is that hooded freak?!" Jack questioned.

"I didn't see him behind us. I'm sure the flames took him."

Glass shattered high above them and Amauros flew out. Giant black wings spread from his back. The robes were gone and he was wearing leather black pants and no shirt. His pale torso reflected from the sunlight. He let out another scream from above. He couldn't see them, but he could hear their terror.

"I AM THE FLAMES!" the words shook the three mens' hearts.

They began to run through the field. Every flap of Amauros' dark wings boomed above them. He was holding a flaming board that must have been torn from the walls.

Amauros landed in front of the three men, and folded his wings. He held the board with his right hand. The men began to backpedal, but they were too late. Amauros grabbed Jack and threw him across the field. An angel flashed from the sky and flew into the blind demon, but Amauros maneuvered him around and smashed the flaming board into his back, sending the angel away in a sizzling light.

"There may be room in Heaven for all, but you three

will spend your time in the agonies of Hell!" He swung the board at Colin. Colin jumped back just barely missing the flames, and fell to his back.

BJ tried to throw a punch, but Amauros caught him in the knees and with a giant swing cracked the jazz man in the skull. Glowing embers flew through the air as BJ was enveloped in flames and vanished.

"NOOO!" Colin screamed. "You son of a bitch!"

Amauros stood above him.

"I wonder what the punishment is for being a coward and a fool?" He said as he raised the weapon over his head.

Jack dove on top of Colin prepared to take the hit. He braced for the flames. Nothing happened.

They looked up to see Amauros motionless, the board midway through the swing. The flames were motionless. The world was still.

The two of them stood up and looked around. The flames and smoke pouring out of the division were frozen. It was as if someone hit the pause button on their world.

"Look!" Jack pointed toward the trees in the distance. A fox was trotting across the field. They chased after it, unsure of what to do once they reached it. The fox stopped and sat in front of them.

"Oh good, the 'heroes' are okay." the fox spoke.

"You can talk?!" Colin asked. He wasn't sure why that surprised him considering all the other crazy shit he had witnessed.

"I can?! Holy shit!" the fox said sarcastically.

"He's kind of an asshole," Jack mentioned.

"You have no idea," a voice came from behind them. It was smooth and creamy and covered in butter: the voice of God.

They turned around to find a golden labradoodle strolling toward them. Its blond locks were shimmering in the sunshine.

"I've seen you before," Colin said.

"So have I," Jack continued.

"I've been around," the dog answered. "I've been keeping tabs on you ever since this blind bastard started making plans to enter Heaven." The dog motioned toward the frozen Duke of Hell.

"Can he hear us?" Colin asked.

"Nah, I stopped time for a minute here. No big deal." Dog answered.

"Okay, so this is probably obvious, but I still need some clarity here. Are you God?" Jack questioned.

"I am."

The two men were both pretty star struck.

"So who is that?" Colin asked toward the fox.

The fox was batting at a wildflower.

"Me?" the fox looked up "Oh, I'm TV's Zak Bagans. You probably recognize me from my hit TV show "Ghost Adventures" on the Travel Channel."

"He's the Devil," God corrected.

"Don't assume my gender..," The fox sighed.

"Are you finally going to fix all of this?!" Colin demanded.

God sat like a good boy and smiled, panting slightly. He looked around at the paused chaos. The flames from the division were motionless. Amauros was in mid strike.

"We created Limbo and Purgatory a long time ago..," God began. "It was supposed to be a sort of autopilot for stewarding souls into their rightful places while we were away."

"Where did you go?"

"I love a good challenge…we had something to work

out," God continued.

"Well, while you two were busy 'working something out' all of these people were attacked and sent to Hell! They passed your stupid tests and still ended up there! Limbo is nothing more than a carrot on a stick." Colin attested.

There were so many questions. Colin wasn't sure what to ask first. He was angry and unsure how to explain it. It wasn't fair. None of this was right. The system was flawed. There's no free will in a world where Limbo and Purgatory exist. Without that, accountability couldn't exist. It was bullshit.

"You're right," God answered.

"You can hear my thoughts?" Colin questioned.

That got Jack's attention.

"Is that really a surprise? Of course I can," the dog responded.

"So you're God, man. Can't you fix all of this with the snap of a finger?" Jack questioned.

"You can do all things, right?!" Colin asked.

"He doesn't like that question," the fox iterated.

The sky darkened and began to rumble.

"Just because I CAN doesn't mean I SHOULD. If I can do all things just through will than the purpose of all things would be null. I CAN do all things, but only through the souls of the world and with love. You are the instruments of my will, and my will is to give all freedom of choice."

The clouds cleared away and the sun came back out. Colin softened his voice.

"Then please explain the purpose of Limbo." Colin wanted an answer.

"Limbo was a temporary fix until the right tools were ready."

"What tools?"

"You two, it seems." God lay down and rolled over. His tail began to wag. "Sometimes I surprise myself."

A leather backpack appeared on the ground next to Jack.

"Whoa…what's this?" Jack stepped toward it.

"It's a treat for you guys," God answered.

"What's in it?" Jack asked.

God looked at Colin. They locked eyes. Colin understood. He picked up the bag and looked inside.

"There's some mac and cheese in here. Oh! And a couple of Fantas," Colin said as he searched through the bag.

The fox's ears perked up.

"Did you say there's a Fanta in there?" the fox asked, "What flavor?" He rolled to his feet and trotted over. Macaroni and cheese and a nice cold Fanta were his absolute favorite treat.

"Grape," Colin answered.

"Grape?" Jack said. He loved that stuff too.

The fox trotted over toward the two.

"I'll trade you," he said to Colin.

"No way. God said this was for us. I'm starving!" Colin said.

"I like Fanta!" the fox told them. "Come on I'll trade you. You can have money…women…fame and fortune!"

"I don't know..," Colin answered.

The fox was desperate.

"I can send you back," he said.

"What?" Jack asked.

"I can send you back to life. Forget about all of this nonsense and go back to the world. You can pick up where you left. The band…who's name I dig by the way. I can give you your life back. Just give me the bag."

Jack looked at Colin.

"I don't know..," Colin seemed unsure.

"Come on! What are you going to do with it? Do you even like Fanta?"

"I love it," Jack said. He reached for the bag.

"No you don't." Colin looked at Jack, his eyes widening as he pulled the bag away.

"What are you talking about? Of course I do."

"You don't remember that conversation where you said you hated Fanta?"

"So I don't like Fanta?" Jack asked.

"No...*remember?*"

"Oh right...yeah I hate it," Jack acknowledged. "Never did care for it, actually."

"Perfect, so give it to me and I'll give you whatever you want," the fox mentioned.

"Well...okay. You have a deal." Colin set the bag down for the fox. He trotted over and poked inside, slowly inching his way in.

"Hey...I don't see any macaro..."

Colin slammed the flaps closed and trapped the fox inside. He began to struggle.

"Hey! This is horse shit! Let me out of this fucking bag!" a muffled Devil cried out.

Colin looked at the dog.

"Now what?"

"There's one more thing to do. If you follow the Euphrates, you'll reach a place that holds a door in this world that once is closed can never be reopened, not even by me. However, it can't be closed until someone is on the other side."

"Who's that?" Colin asked

"He's in that bag."

"Don't assume my gender!" the fox yelled from the

bag.

"You need to take him to Janus, who guards the door. He will know what to do. The game is over, Devil."

The Devil heard this and knew that the bet that was made long ago had just been lost. The fox that no one could trap just trapped itself. And there was no Fanta. It wasn't a good day for him...or her.

"What about all of this?" Colin asked as he pointed to the chaos.

"Everything will be corrected."

"What about him?" Jack asked pointing at Amauros.

"He is probably going to be angry when you leave," God answered.

"You can't just keep him like this? Or blow him up or put him in some kind of jail or something?"

"It doesn't work that way. Best I can do is give you a head start."

The dog circled a few times and lay back down.

Colin and Jack stood there. *Surely there is someone better suited for this than me?* He thought.

"You two are the only ones left," God answered.

God damn it...I forgot he knows what I'm thinking.

"Easy now."

Sorry.

"It's fine. The river is east of here. Better get to it. And no Jack, you aren't a zombie."

"Poltergeist." Jack said to himself.

FORTY-ONE

The Euphrates seemed to barely move as the three walked along the banks. Jack had a short sleeve yellow button up on. He couldn't remember where he found it. Colin was still barefoot and carrying the Devil on his back. It was a black leather backpack with flaps that swung as they walked. Occasionally, the fox would move around inside, but other than the ultimate force of darkness on board, it was a peaceful walk.

"Everyone is in Hell, and I have the Devil in a backpack," Colin said as they continued.

"Sucks, man," Jack responded.

"I think I'm in shock. Am I in shock?"

"Snap out of it man! We're fine. We're gonna throw this little dude through that door and everything will be fine."

"HA!" the fox said through muffles.

"Shut up!" they both yelled at the bag.

"Okay…but you can't trust him. He's a trickster," the fox answered.

They ignored him.

"If you let me go I will free every single soul in Hell," the fox said again. "Scout's honor."

"Why on earth would we believe you? Or even want to help you. You're the Devil. The WORST." Colin scoffed.

"Yeah!" Jack followed up.

"Don't drink the Kool-Aid, man. I've been misrepresented since the dawn of man! All I ever wanted was free love, baby. I'm a lover, not a fighter."

They again ignored him.

"Okay, answer me this then: if God loved all of his children so much, then why did he abandon them for so long? All for some silly challenge against me? If that's true then, well, I hate to say it, but maybe it's not love that he feels for you all."

"What would it be then?" Jack responded.

"I don't know…I'm just spitballing here. Ownership?" the backpack said again.

"Ownership?" Jack again gave in to the conversation.

"It seems to me…and this is just my perspective…but it seems to me that he feels like people are more like pets. Maybe even worse…like animals in a zoo."

They came to a bridge and crossed the river. More and more trees began to appear. It was full of foliage and beautiful flowers. They had never seen such flora. A rabbit darted across the path in front of them. They followed deeper into the garden.

"You'd say anything to get out of that bag," Colin answered.

"He's got a point, though," Jack said. "I mean why put all of us through the torment when you have the ability to take care of us?"

"There's more to it than that," Colin answered.

"Not the way I see it. There are too many stupid rules in the world and we're expected to just blindly follow them and watch as others, who probably don't even DESERVE it, have easier lives?" the fox said.

"You're not 'us,'" Colin said with frustration.

"Yeah but he's right. Shitty people have great lives and great people struggle...or worse! They get sick and die! Why would God create cancer?!"

"YEAH?!" the Devil agreed.

"And I also think that there is nothing wrong with free love," Jack continued.

"Let a hoe be a hoe! That's my motto from the grotto," the Devil again agreed.

"It's no different than being put in jail for weed! God grew it!"

"Toke toke pass, bitches!" the Devil yet again agreed.

"We can't have this argument right now," Colin pleaded with Jack.

"You probably still believe in Santa Claus, huh?" the fox said.

"You may have been my Watcher back in Limbo, but who's watching who now?" Jack was getting frustrated.

They moved into a clearing. There were birds chirping in the distance. Stars were visible in the clear blue sky. It was paradise.

They saw something on a nearby hill. It was an enormous door, barely cracked open.

"There," Colin pointed out. He began to walk up the hill.

"Maybe life isn't supposed to be fair, man. Maybe that's what makes it so great when it's great? I don't know, man. I'm not a philosopher. I'm just some dead farmer with the devil in a bag that God told me to banish to Hell. All I know is that everyone that I care about is, at this moment, in Hell being deep fried or beaten or stuck in a room with skunks or something. Can we please get this over with? Cause it's been weird and I'm tired."

"Let's let him out, and he'll set everyone free?" Jack

insisted.

"We can't trust him!"

"He's got no reason to lie!"

"He's the fricking Devil, man!"

They didn't notice the two faced man leaning against the tree. He was eight feet tall and wearing long green robes. One of his faces was wearing glasses and he was focused on a Sudoku puzzle. The other face noticed the two men approach and he grabbed the flaming sword that was leaning against a rock.

He stood up before them and interrupted the argument.

"I have been waiting for a very long time," he began.

"Are you...Janus?" Colin asked.

"It's pronounce 'Jah ness', not 'Jay ness.' Damn. God told you that didn't he? He always calls me that."

"Boy, that God is just a nice fella," Jack mentioned.

"Not helping my case here, Janus," Colin said. "Can we just give this to you and get this door closed?"

He held out the bag. The fox was scurrying around inside.

"I was expecting him to be a lot bigger," Janus said. He had been waiting at this doorway for thousands of years, eager to finally do his duty. He had so many plans once his shift was over. He was thinking Cancun.

"Well, I'm not surprised by much anymore," Colin answered. He took the bag off of his shoulders.

Janus walked toward them. He reached his hands out.

"I'm sorry, Colin...but I don't think this is the right move," Jack said sullenly before snagging the bag out of his hands.

"WHAT ARE YOU DOING?!" Colin fought back and the two began wrestling over the bag. The fox was screaming inside.

"Stop! I'm going to throw up!" the Devil yelled.

A shadow flew over them and they both looked up to see Amauros descending on them. He kicked Colin so hard he flew into the bushes. Jack took a hard punch to the jaw and left him dazed. The bag was tossed nearly twenty feet across the clearing. The fox reached his paws out of the flap and was desperately trying to unhook the clasp and free himself.

Janus attacked the blind Duke of Hell from behind. Amauros sensed the movement and threw the two faced guardian aside using his own momentum. Janus swung his flaming sword backwards missing the duke by inches. Amauros delivered a jab to one of Janus' faces and bloodied his nose.

Jack shook off the punch and looked around for the bag. He stood up and ran toward it. Colin dove on top of it before Jack could reach it.

"WE HAVE TO DO THIS!" Colin pleaded as they wrestled for the bag.

Janus swung his sword again but the Duke of Hell evaded, this time with a kick to the ribs. Janus tumbled down the hill. He landed on his sword. The flaming blade stuck out of his back and Janus slumped to the ground.

Amauros spread his dark wings and flew on top of the two men. He stomped on Colin's arm causing him to scream out in pain. Jack was on Amauros' back trying to gouge his eyes, but it had no effect. Amauros fluttered a wing and sent Jack tumbling away. He picked up the backpack with the devil inside.

"No!" Colin yelled.

Amauros opened the bag and the fox poked his head out. They stood in front of the gate.

The fox began to laugh.

"You fools! I'm the Lord of Darkness. You think

some pansy ass farmer and a burnout songwriter are going to be able to stop me?! Of course not! I'm eternal damnation personified! I shake the very bones of man! What did you think that you wer…"

Amauros threw the bag through the doorway.

"WHAT THE FUUUUUCKKK..!" the Devil yelled as he disappeared into his banishment.

"I'm the Lord of Darkness, now." Amauros went to close the door, but then stopped and turned toward Colin.

"You…" He began toward him.

Colin was on his back. He started crab walking backwards away from Amauros.

"You have ruined everything!" he said. His barren eyes lit up with rage.

He grabbed the Watcher by the leg and began dragging him toward the door.

"You tried to take everything from me!" he snarled.

Jack ran to help his friend. He dove into Amauros' legs.

"All of my work nearly wasted because of two pathetic losers!!" the duke screamed as he backhanded Jack, knocking him away.

Colin tried to grab on to something but all he could find damp grass. It tore from the ground as he held on.

"You can join him in pit!" He swung back to throw Colin through the doorway. Jack slid behind them and grabbed Colin's hands and with his feet dug into the earth pulled him back from the momentum. It gave them enough time to notice something was approaching.

A horrible bellow came from the sky. A thunderous booming from the wings of what could only be a creature of power and nobility, echoed throughout the garden. The silhouette broke through the sunlight and a mighty creature flew toward them.

"HANK?!" Jack couldn't believe it. "It's Hank!"

Hank, the Demon Camel of Capite, flew with the tenacity of a fighter pilot and barreled into Amauros freeing Colin from his grip. Hank flew back into the sky and turned to make his second run. His shrieking echoed through the skies of paradise.

Amauros jumped back from the ground and was ready to fight back, but was dazed from the tumble.

Colin watched in amazement as hordes of Hellish creatures appeared from the surrounding forest. His recent friend, and suicidal hillbilly, Wade, led the insurrection.

Amauros spread his wings in defiance.

"TRAITORS!" he screamed with all of his strength.

The demons began toward him.

"We're done taking orders from you," Jared yelled from the back. He was done brown nosing.

Wade spoke up, "We have all decided to accept our fate. We know what we did. We're ready to do our time. Purgatory is over."

"This is my destiny! I won't let you cowards steal this from me!" Amauros replied. He charged and began to fight viciously. He sent creatures flying into the trees, three and four at a time. A creature jumped on his back. He effortlessly spread his black wings and sent the demon tumbling.

Jack ran over and helped Colin to his feet. There was no need for apologies.

"We have to do something!" Jack said.

"Has the door been closed?!" Colin asked, catching his breath.

They glanced over to see the door to the enormous gateway swinging in the breeze. It was never shut.

"I have a very stupid idea," Colin said.

"That should be written on my tombstone," Jack smiled.

Amauros grabbed one of the demons and began using him as a blunt weapon. Bones cracked as he swung the poor soul through the air connecting with the skulls of the surrounding monsters.

Wade approached him from the side and dove into the duke's legs. Amauros lost his balance and dropped the weaponized creature, who landed with a lifeless thud. The blind monster threw a hard punch to Wade, knocking him unconscious.

"HEY!" Colin yelled. He was standing in front of the gateway, holding the flaming sword. It was heavy in his hands.

Amauros turned toward the Watcher and burned with rage. There were no words to surmise his anger. He screamed into the sky, spread his wings, and launched himself up the hill toward Colin.

Colin pointed the sword at Amauros, poised to swing it. He knew he would only have one chance at making this work. Everything came down to this moment, and Colin surprised himself at how calm and collected he was. He was focused and unafraid. It felt good.

Amauros reached the top of the hill and was barreling toward Colin at full speed. He held his arms back, prepared to throw Colin through the gate and finish this. He'd deal with his friend afterwards. His eyes lit up, and he locked into the sound of the rain bouncing off of Colin's shoulders.

Everything felt like it was moving in slow motion. Colin watched the creature's fist moving toward his face. He turned to look at Jack, who was running toward them. They made eye contact. *Life is too short for regrets. I ain't gonna die with a full tank of gas.* Jack's words echoed in Colin's head. He looked back at Amauros and waited for the right moment.

As Amauros threw the punch he didn't even bother to put his feet on the ground. He was putting his entire force behind it. Colin closed his eyes and placed the blade of the fiery sword against his own forehead. The flames engulfed him instantly, and with a flash he disappeared. Amauros' fist flew through where Colin's face had been a second before and he threw himself into the gate. He caught himself by the door, but Jack was there before he could regain his balance. Jack jumped feet first into Amauros' back, sending him falling into the swirling darkness on the other side. Amauros screamed with rage as he disappeared into the pit. There would be no return for him, nor the Devil. They just had the rest of eternity looking up from the bottom and would never be able to leave that place again.

Jack slammed the door shut. He could hear a click from an unseen lock. At once, the skies cleared up, and the sun shone through the clouds. The smell of the rain brought calm. Jack looked up at the sky.

FORTY-TWO

Jack was helping Wade limp back toward Limbo. The Euphrates was running faster than before, moving the rain water off toward some other distant, perhaps stranger, world.

"Where's Colin? What happened?" Wade questioned. He had missed Colin zapping himself with the flaming sword. He had missed Amauros being banished. He had missed Jack's badass ninja-like moves.

"Colin...he's gone. He tricked that blind bastard into the doorway. He just went up in flames and vanished."

Wade was speechless.

"How did you manage all of this?" Jack pointed down toward the demons walking among them. They were slowly starting to return to their original form, unsure of where to go now that they had quit their jobs.

"I stayed behind. I started breaking people out, ya know? So eventually there was a small group....did you know that beast from the field fucks his couch?"

"Really?"

"Yeah. I'll never unsee it. Crazy. Anyway, eventually there was a small group of us and we began to split up. Before long, there was a large amount of us escapees. It was a rush! So we eventually made our way to Purgatory, and it wasn't that hard to convince the pushers to do the right thing. They're not all bad. Don't get me wrong, a lot of them are real pieces of horsecrap. But most just did the best they could with the life they were given."

Jack nodded. He could relate. He had been to Hell, and part of him felt that he deserved it. The more he thought about it, the more he realized that most of the people he knew, if not all of them, didn't deserve Heaven or Hell. People aren't cartoons. Life is so much more complicated than that.

*   *   *   *   *

Colin was on his back. He opened his eyes to darkness. Smoke was still floating off of his arms and legs from the blaze he had gone up in. The top of his head looked as though he had just taken off a stocking cap in the middle of the Antarctic. There was no light, but he could see himself. There was nothing.

"Colin," a voice echoed throughout the darkness.

He was tired. He really didn't have the mental capacity to deal with another oddball situation. Dark, swirling, nothingness was fine for the moment. He ignored the voice.

"Colin...?" the voice asked again. It was a deep, powerful voice.

Colin rolled over on his side and closed his eyes. He just wanted to sleep.

"I know you're awake...I'm not going to stop."

Colin stayed silent.

"Colin Colin Colin Colin Colin Colin Colin Co..."

"OH MY GOD! WHAT?!?!" Colin reacted.

"Well excuse me, Mr. Grumpyballs. I didn't mean to

interrupt your all important self-pity nap. It's just me, the Lord of all things here, but we can be on your schedule." The voice responded.

Colin rubbed his temples, "I'm sorry. What's up?"

"Grumplestiltskin."

Colin sighed, "I'm sorry." He stood up and patted the smoke from his arms.

"Where am I? What happened?" He asked the void before him.

"Do you ever think about time? It's just a big circle, you know?" the Lord responded.

"I did not know that. I didn't really study space-time quantum theories as a child."

"Think of a wheel…Life is a highway, and people are going to ride it all night long. I love that song. But seriously, time is a wheel. Life as you know it exists on the tread. It's rolling along a racetrack, and occasionally there are a few bumps here and there, but it's moving forward as far you know. Right now, we are in the center bore of time: the middle of the wheel."

"Okay…"

"Well occasionally, in order to continue the race, the driver needs to make a pit stop. Check the engine, make sure there's oil and all that stuff."

"You're losing me."

"Well, creation is a never ending process. I try different approaches, but people are so incredible. There's always another surprise. You're right, you know? Limbo takes away from real choice. Where's the accountability in that? I was so busy with the Devil's challenge that I just put things on autopilot."

"So you're going to get rid of Limbo?"

"I'm saying that we are in a pit stop right now…but I think we should take another lap."

"Another lap? What does that mean?" Colin questioned?

"Thank you, Colin," the voice faded away.

Colin felt an intense fatigue coming on. His hands became numb. His eyelids became heavy. He had trouble breathing. He decided to lie back down. There was a subtle pain in his chest. A bright light came on from above and slowly washed over him. He closed his eyes, and once again Colin Lodestar fell softly into darkness.

FORTY-THREE

2018

Jack's short sleeved, preshrunk, regular fit, Wrangler button up was missing four buttons. This left it a total of three, however, Jack only needed two. He liked his chest to be able to breathe, especially when he was shopping.

The pawn shop was quiet amongst the many patrons. Jack was at the counter looking at the guitars that hung from the wall. He had been in this store many times to sell off some old junk in order to make the rent, but today he was here to spend.

The Devil Wears Nada had just released their third album, *Demon Camel*, and it was getting some fantastic recognition around the region. Things were going well, and he thought today would be a good day to scope out some engagement rings, under the guise of guitar shopping. As he was searching through the box he found one. It was a modest ring, but it looked like an antique. It was odd and beautiful. *She would want a ring with more story than diamond.* He hoped it was the right size. The clerk approached him and Jack bought the ring as secretly as possible.

"Jack, look at all of these records!" Olivia called to him from the other side of the shop.

Jack shoved the ring in his pocket and walked over to join her. They began scrolling the records, laughing at some of the outdated album covers. He came across an old jazz album and picked it up. It was an older pressing, the date from the recording read 1955.

"*The Twins: Live at Massey Hall,*" Jack read out loud. He had a strange desire come over him. He had to have it.

"I think I'm going to buy this," he said.

"Jazz?" Olivia asked him. "You've never owned a jazz album."

"I don't know why, but I feel… connected to this." Jack decided.

Olivia smiled and gave him a kiss on the cheek. "Let me buy it for you," she said.

The two walked up to the counter and she handed over the money. It was a warm morning in sunny Colorado, and a melodic *ding* rang in the air as the two exited the pawn shop. They hopped into Jack's blue 1999 Ford Econoline, started the engine, merged on I-70 and headed west toward Lookout Mountain.

1971.

"RUN!" someone yelled. The glow from the bonfire went out suddenly.

Colin helped Anna to her feet. They spun around to meet one of Anna's friends stumbling through the pebbles toward them.

"Cops!" she yelled to them. Colin's heart sunk into his stomach. He was in some major trouble.

"Shit! We have to run!" Anna said.

Before they knew it a herd of high school students were scrambling toward the creek. The splashes were somewhat muted by the running water as they began to jump in and swim across to the other side. Colin realized that the only way out was to run from the police.

"COME ON!" Anna said. She held out her hand.

"I can't run from the police! My folks will kill me!" Colin argued.

"If I DON'T run from the police my folks will kill me!" Anna said. "Come on! They'll never catch us!"

"I...I can't." Colin said.

"Take my hand, Colin. We will be fine," she said calmly with her hand held toward him.

Flashlights started peering down the path and the sound of the officers walkie talkies were floating through the surrounding trees.

"Colin..," Anna said with disappointment.

He looked into her eyes. He never wanted this moment to end. Anna stood there waiting. He had to make a decision.

"Let's go!" Colin grabbed her hand and ran to the water's edge. They both dove into the creek together, giggling the whole way across. As they got out on the other end, they saw the police reach the opposite bank.

Colin smiled as he took Anna's hand. He helped her to her feet, and they took off into the woods together. The laughter continued as Colin Lodestar ran softly toward a future that only he would shape.

The End.

ABOUT THE AUTHOR

Limbo is Adam's first novel. He lives in Duluth, Minnesota and is also a musician and songwriter. He invites readers to contact him on Twitter and Instagram @tsdoors or email him at adamherman12@gmail.com.

Made in the USA
Monee, IL
08 August 2020